Cathy & Chris Under Siege

MARK DAYDY

This is a work of fiction. All names, characters, locations and incidents are products of the author's imagination, or have been used fictitiously. Any resemblance to actual persons living or dead, locales, or events is entirely coincidental. No part of this book may be reproduced without prior written permission from the author.

Copyright © 2019 MARK DAYDY

All rights reserved

ISBN: 9781797540719

Cover design by MIKE DAYDY

CONTENTS

1.	A Time For Action	1
2.	Behind The Bookcase	9
3.	Um… About The Castle	15
4.	Those Plans You Had…?	22
5.	Still Waters	31
6.	Connections	37
7.	Business As Usual	46
8.	Tyler	55
9.	Family Trees	62
10.	Down by the Canal	71
11.	Knowledge is Power	81
12.	Attention Citizens!	91
13.	A Little History	96
14.	Can I Count On Your Support?	104
15.	How To Beat Shane Tyler	112
16.	A Fresh Approach	121
17.	It's Like This…	128
18.	Here's An Idea	138
19.	The People's Festival	145
20.	The Lure	154

21. Waterside	160
22. Muniments	168
23. Inspiration Strikes	179
24. The Dream	187
25. Farewells...?	192
26. Spies	201
27. Into Battle	207
28. Well, I Never!	216
29. Now What?	220
30. A Place in the World	225
A Note From The Author	233

1

A Time For Action

Just before lunchtime on a Monday in late March, British Heritage site manager Cathy Chappell left 12th Century De Gaul Castle's rear tower and entered the courtyard. As ever, she was inspired by a history of Norman knights, mediaeval monks, and burly sword-makers... and not quite so inspired by the temporary porta-loos and rotting 19th Century structure that housed her office.

"Ugh, what a dump."

She felt free to judge. After all, her family built the castle almost nine centuries ago. At least, that's what her grandad told anyone who cared to listen. In truth, she didn't believe his tall tales – although, weirdly, during the past few months she *had* begun to feel a deeper connection to the old place, one that seemed to transcend her job of looking after it.

"Possible news," said Kay, emerging from the office. As ever, a pony tail restrained her wild chestnut hair while on duty. "Melanie Sanchez just called saying something big might be happening – then Stewart called her to a meeting."

"Right," said Cathy. "No doubt she'll get back to us."

"Oh, and the computer's updating."

"Great…"

With Kay heading off to another part of the castle, Cathy paused before the office. As ever, she tried to ignore the horrible green door and decrepit window beside it. Then, stepping up to the threshold, she tried to ignore the drab buttery décor and faint smell of damp within.

Oh, for a nice office instead of this…

'This' being a sizeable but soulless space with a dark, heavy-duty bookcase taking up most of the left-hand wall; her ancient, rickety desk facing the far wall alongside a door to a small, unused, windowless room beyond; and a right-hand wall brightened only by a couple of De Gaul Castle posters. There were prison recreation rooms with more style.

Cathy crossed the hideous russet carpet and took her seat at the desk facing the wall. The computer's on-screen message stated 'Update 99% Complete', prompting Cathy to reckon she might have to wait another Ice Age for the pile of junk to finish its business.

Firing hate rays at the frustrating machine, she wondered if the time had come to put it on display alongside the castle's mediaeval torture devices. After all, it was almost old enough and it often made people scream in anguish.

"Meant to show you…" said Kay returning to the office.

Cathy turned to behold Kay's phone displaying yet another photo of six-month-old niece Fleur.

"Adorable or what?" said Kay. "It makes me feel like

rushing out and getting pregnant. The miracle of life, eh?"
Cathy smiled and turned back to the computer.
"Ah, speaking of miracles, the computer's finished loading."
"There's a video too," said Kay.
Cathy half turned again to watch baby Fleur dribble.
"Have you and Chris not thought of it?" asked Kay. *What, climbing the Himalayas, swimming the Atlantic, going to Mars?*
"Not really, Kay."
"You'd make great parents. I can tell."
"I'm sure we'd be terrible."
Baby Fleur started to cry and the video ended abruptly. Cathy smiled again and Kay departed to get on with her work.
A baby crying.
That always got to her.
Cathy buried the ache of not being able to have children. She was at De Gaul Castle to work.
Need to do something.
She stood and checked the staff roster pinned to the wall. Entering the last week of March, she had two paid seasonal assistants including Kay, and seven volunteers down for duty shifts. She'd have to find a couple more volunteers for the height of summer – although perhaps not the eighty-year-old woman who popped in last week claiming to be William the Conqueror's re-incarnated wife, Matilda of Flanders.

Cathy peered into the little mirror on the wall beside the roster. She'd put it there to check her teeth for bits of lettuce or to remove a smudge of dirt on her face before stepping outside among visitors. Right now her carefree auburn hair looked in need of a stylist, but her brown eyes were surprisingly clear and alert for a Monday.

Seven years. That's how long she and Chris had been trying. In half that time, Tina at the London office had met Mitch, married him, bought a house, had a daughter, split up, sold the house, found a new partner, and was expecting again.

Need to do something positive.

She sat down.

Determined to drag an important Leicestershire tourist attraction into the 21st Century, she thought of getting on with typing up yet another achievable, fully-costed plan for the castle. But no. Not only would the word processor freeze at the second bullet point, it was hard to get stuck in with a constant icy draft on her neck, a deep shadow cast by her head over the computer keyboard, and a damp, crumbling, paint-resistant wall constituting the view from her wobbly desk.

Need to do something active!

Cathy rose sharply, sending her chair scuttling backwards on squeaky castors across the decaying carpet.

"Count to ten, Cathy… this is still the dream job. It just needs damp-proofing."

She got to five then stopped. Her twelve-month temporary posting to the castle from London was something she'd requested at a time British Heritage was planning to reorganize the random regional setups. But Cathy had a secret plan to make it permanent, involving sneak visits to the adjoining region run by soon-to-retire Pete Williams, because taking charge of two regions would be Cathy's passport to a permanent job in the Midlands.

"The flush is stuck again!" Kay yelled from outside.

Cathy peered out through the ill-fitting rotten window to Kay waving from the ladies porta-loo doorway across the courtyard. The porta-loos were only meant to be there until sufficient funds could be raised to renovate the toilets in the 1940s army-built lean-to that was currently hidden behind said porta-loos. As things stood, after six years in situ, the temporary toilets were in danger of becoming a British Heritage tourist attraction in their own right.

Thank God Australian businessman Mr Hall had promised to put some money in. He'd been up to the castle a few times over the past month and seemed keen to help. Maybe his generosity would even stretch to a new office...?

But no – Cathy was reluctant to spend money on anything not related to maintaining the castle's original structure or improving the visitor experience.

Turning back to her desk, she wondered when she might get down to some serious castle-related work. She wanted the rear tower roof repaired so that its upper floor could be re-opened to the public after eight years. She also wanted to move the mediaeval weaponry display from the main hall to the rear tower so that the main hall could become a spacious meeting area. The meeting area was currently in the banqueting hall, which housed movable, ugly bright green plastic tables and chairs. Although they didn't serve food, Cathy wanted to improve the banqueting hall with high quality, sympathetic seating. She liked the idea of people bringing packed lunches to eat where knights had eaten many centuries before them. Instead of all that, Cathy needed to contact the porta-loo and damp-proof people, and find a way to smarten up the office without spending a penny.

Although...

An idea began to form. When it came to the office, maybe she didn't need cash – just a bit of lateral thinking.

On a whim, she grabbed the edge of the desk and

began dragging it away from the wall – until a leg fell off, tipping the whole thing violently to one side. Grabbing the computer and keyboard, she could only watch as the screen, mouse, stapler, phone, pen tidy, mug, and two thousand tourist information leaflets slid off and crashed to the floor.

"You okay, Cath?" said Kay, appearing at the door.

"The desk's possessed by an evil spirit."

"So that's why it's trying to walk across the office."

"Could you get an axe from the weaponry display?"

"Now, now, Cathy, before we make firewood of it, let's see if we can keep costs down by sticking the leg back in."

"Okay, but let's turn it to face the other way. I'm fed up having my back to the door. It's only a matter of time before Sammy the Serial Killer creeps in while I'm posting on Facebook."

Together, they pulled the desk away from the wall and turned it to face the door and window.

"That looks better," said Cathy.

This was Kay's cue to wedge the errant leg back into place.

"Now you can say hi to Sammy as he comes in."

"Thanks, Kay."

The two of them soon had the mess cleared up, but Cathy wasn't finished.

"How about rearranging all the other top-of-the-range office accessories?" she suggested.

"Okay."

Kay grabbed the rickety metal tea trolley that supported the printer and pulled it a few feet to the window.

"Right, what else?" she asked.

"Hello, big boy," said Cathy. She was eyeing up the

solid hardwood book case that took up most of one wall.
"I'm guessing you didn't come as a flat pack."
"That's probably a move too far," said Kay.
"I'm sure we could handle it," said Cathy.
She assessed the sheer size of the thing, and then moved in closer to examine some book spines.
"*Military Fitness Manual... Camping in Winter... Rifle Range Regulations 1947...*"
"Dear old Henry," said Kay. "He loved books."
"I love books, too. Just not these books."
"A proper army man, he was. Well, National Service, which you couldn't avoid in those days."
"He must have felt at home working here," said Cathy, heading for her newly-positioned chair.

She didn't have anything against Henry Hume, her predecessor who had recently retired after thirty-two years at De Gaul – even if he had spent their changeover week disagreeing with all of her ideas on the basis that they were new. But Henry's rule was over and, with the Easter holidays almost upon them, Cathy wanted to sweep away all of his boring, tourist-repelling initiatives and put the region's best Norman castle on the 'Must Visit' list of anyone who came within fifty miles of it.

She eyed the bookcase again.

"How about if we move it to the back wall? At least then it'll be behind me and I can pretend I'm not sitting in front of the world's dullest book collection. We could put a couple of pictures in its place... and maybe a rubber plant."

"We'd better clear it then," said Kay.

They started unloading the shelves and stacking *Games for Army Cadets, Studying Semaphore, Makeshift Lethal Weapons* and all the others on the floor by the opposite wall.

"Here's a good one," said Kay. "*Cooking For Fifty Men*. To think I've been wasting time feeding potential boyfriends one at a time."

Cathy laughed – she liked working with Kay.

Once all the dust-related sneezing was over and all the dull volumes were piled up on the floor, Cathy and Kay took hold of the bookcase.

'Right," said Kay. "Hopefully it's not nailed down."

'Right," said Cathy. "Three, two, one…"

"Urghhhhhhhhhh!"

They paused, gasping. Then Cathy checked the gap they had opened up.

"Three inches," she puffed. "Not bad. We should be there by nightfall."

"Right," said Kay. "Three, two, one…"

"Urghhhhhhhhh!"

They paused again, panting and regretting the absence of an Olympic weightlifting team hanging around in the courtyard.

Cathy checked the gap again.

"That has *got* to be five inches," she wheezed, sounding like an old boiler.

"Six," rasped Kay, taking a look. "I instinctively know the difference between five and six inches. Please don't ask me how."

Cathy puffed out a laugh as she peered as far as possible into the dusty gap. And that's when she noticed something unexpected.

2

Behind The Bookcase

Chris Chappell came marching up the grassy hill almost nine centuries after a certain visitor did likewise – with the intention of talking persuasively with the castle's occupant. Only, the mediaeval caller received an arrow in the gut and fell at the exact spot on which Chris's next step landed.

Of course, Chris carried no mediaeval weapons – just cheese salad baguettes and apple drinks in a carrier bag.

His intention?

To deliver them to the castle and then go fishing on the canal.

The danger?

Cathy would not be happy at him spending time fishing on a Monday. Hence the need to talk persuasively, along the lines of using fishing as a vehicle for pondering ways to attract more clients to his copywriting and web design business.

He ran a hand through his unruly dark brown hair and

smoothed down his green and black striped rugby shirt. He'd worked for a client over the weekend and into Monday morning, hadn't he? And you couldn't fish on the canal at the weekend unless you wanted to be disturbed by other people getting out and enjoying the fresh air. But Monday afternoons were different. The canal tow-path would be as God intended – quiet.

Up ahead, on top of the hill, the castle looked great. It always did from a distance. It just looked less great the nearer you got. Of course, he was becoming an expert now. When they first arrived, just before Christmas, that pile of stones was simply a castle. Now he knew the big bit at the front was the keep and the raised bit it stood on, the motte. A curtain wall encircled a courtyard, or bailey, behind it. There was also a separate tower at the back end of the bailey. Noticeably, two big sections of the original curtain wall had vanished – having fallen down in 1455 and 1680 and subsequently been stolen by the mayor to help replace the wooden town hall that collapsed during the Great Storm of 1703.

Chris scanned the upper windows of the keep. He didn't believe in Kay's legend of some ghost walking around up there, but he was always relieved when he didn't spot anyone peering back at him.

He pushed on, puffing a little.

"Come on, you're thirty-three, not ninety-three," he told himself.

He put a lack of fitness down to his profession, which involved sitting down a lot. That's why he needed to get out fishing, so he could sit down in a different location. Then he'd have more time to ponder not just client-attracting strategies but also ways in which to get fit that didn't involve giving up pies and beer.

Of course, fitness was important. He knew that. There

were people in America who bolted laptops to their running machines so they could jog and hold Skype meetings at the same time. But Chris couldn't envisage that for himself. He liked to ponder a bit – and you couldn't do that on a running machine or you might be struck by inspiration, stop running, and be shot backwards into a wall.

He pressed on, upward to the castle gate, which stood inside a big arched entrance in the keep. It was accessed by walking up a long ramp overlooked by slit windows made for archers – as if 12th Century Normans didn't trust visitors.

For Chris, the main thing was having Cathy sorted and happy. He loved her dearly but she was easier to live with when fully engaging her passions – and you certainly needed passion to work in a cold, damp old ruin. Not that Cathy had expected an easy time. They both knew it would be tough for her to raise the money needed to prevent a crumbling castle from falling into further disrepair. What Cathy hadn't foreseen was the endless nonsense completely unrelated to protecting and showcasing Norman history.

Still, she loved it. That much he knew.

And they had their agreement in place. It was a temporary posting, but with Cathy's long-shot plan to turn temporary into permanent. If it worked, then great – they would stay in Castle Hill. If it failed, she would return to the British Heritage HQ in London, content that she'd tried her best. Either way, Chris would be happy, although a return to London did seem to be the most likely outcome. That's why he wasn't getting too involved at Castle Hill.

Off to his right, a young mother was playing ball with her toddler. Chris smiled at them.

"Soon be playing for England," he called.

What a shame, he thought. What a bloody crying shame they were unable to have children. What a rotten con-trick of Nature that his lovely wife would never be able to take their own child fishing, go-karting or spend time kicking a ball around in a pretend cup final. He wished for it too, of course, more than he might care to say. Cathy was always telling him how he shouldn't bottle up emotions. Experts were always saying how you should talk about these things, but, for Chris, they had talked and talked and talked and sometimes he just felt all talked out.

He sniffed up a lungful of fresh air and carried on up the hill. It was almost lunchtime and those sandwiches were required. No doubt Cathy and Kay were dribbling wrecks. He could only pray they would forgive him for forgetting to bring any chocolate.

He paused at the old arched gateway and eyed the crack that ran diagonally from the apex of the arch to the top right corner of the stone edifice. It would take more than a tube of Polyfilla to fix that lot.

He marched in through the gateway and headed for the office, which was situated to the right against a brick wall that had replaced missing Norman stone. He liked the courtyard. Ignoring the porta-loos, the Victorian office, and the slightly older bit alongside the office that acted as a storage unit, he could imagine peasants coming to beg for mercy for failing to produce enough wheat or virgin daughters for the feudal master.

"Morning ladies," he began as he entered the office.

Any further words of greeting came to a halt as he took in Cathy puffing and sweating, the desk in the wrong place, and the bookcase partly pulled away from the wall.

"Cathy's got a bee in her bonnet," said Kay.

"That's not good," said Chris, putting the carrier bag

on the desk. "It usually turns into a whole swarm of bees that has everyone running for cover."

"We found something," said Cathy.

"Behind the bookcase," said Kay.

Chris detected a manly moment coming up. To carry it off, he'd need to look cool about poking his head behind the bookcase – not that he fancied peering through cobwebs at a dead rat or, worse, a live rat.

"What are you waiting for?" asked Cathy.

He peered behind.

"There's nothing there," he declared, somewhat relieved.

"Try looking harder," said Cathy.

"I am. There's still nothing there. Apart from that door."

"Eureka," said Cathy.

"Why is there a door behind the bookcase?" Chris asked.

"No idea," said Cathy, "but now you're here, let's get the bookcase moved so we can take a proper look."

"It's a big old thing," Chris mused. "Are you sure it was designed to be moved – and I'm including by earthquake or direct nuclear strike…?"

"Chris, you're six foot and thirteen stone," said Cathy. "Just grab hold."

All three of them took hold.

"Three, two, one…"

"Urghhhhhhhhh!" they gasped.

"There's not an elephant sitting on top, is there?" said Chris.

"And again," said Cathy.

"Urghhhhhhhh!"

It took a few goes before the bookcase was shunted far enough from the wall to properly give access to the hidden door – a solid-looking hardwood specimen finished in peeled varnish.

Chris gathered his wits, took a steadying breath, brushed away the cobwebs, and moved in to try the dull brass handle.

"It's locked," he announced. "Do you have a key?"

"Yes," said Cathy. "It's on a chain around my neck."

"Really?"

"Chris, we didn't know we had a door, so the chances of me having a key are slim."

"You definitely didn't know there was a door then?" Chris asked Kay.

"That bookcase hasn't moved an inch in the time I've worked here. It must lead into the back of the old storage area, which is weird."

"Why's it weird?" said Chris.

"There isn't a door at the back of the old storage area."

"Are you sure?" said Cathy. "The storage area is filled floor to ceiling with junk. Has anyone even seen the back wall?"

"Well, no," said Kay, "but I'm sure there isn't a door there."

Chris sighed. He hated it when mysterious doors got in the way of a spot of fishing.

3

Um... About The Castle

The phone on the desk rang.

"That had better be the porta-loo people," said Cathy, "or we might have to start digging latrines."

She picked up the phone.

"De Gaul Castle. Cathy Chappell speaking."

"Hi Cathy, it's Melanie Sanchez. How are you?"

'Melanie, hi. I'm fine." Cathy had worked with Melanie at the British Heritage London office before moving to Castle Hill. "We just found a locked secret door."

"Wow, that sounds cool."

"Well, possibly not. It might lead to the back of the storage area. Although Kay doesn't think so."

"Do let me know if you find a stash of gold behind it."

"Absolutely. I'll get my butler to text you from my private tropical island."

"That's all sounds perfectly reasonable, Cathy."

"On other matters, Kay said you might have some news."

"Yes, well... have you heard anything your end?"

"About what?"

"It's not official yet – I mean it's all pretty hush-hush and I'm not meant to know. I just happened to overhear one of the board members on his phone in the pub..."

"And?"

"I think there's going to be a press release at some point, but... I mean I can't say for certain, and it's not confirmed..."

"Spit it out, Mel."

"They're selling the castle."

"What castle?"

"De Gaul."

Cathy's heart missed a beat.

"What??"

"That's what I heard, Cath. Don't quote me on it. I'm only admin."

Cathy felt time and space move weirdly around her, as if she were being ejected from the normal world into a parallel reality.

"Mel, they can't sell the castle. It's a national treasure." She flashed a glance at Kay and Chris, who looked as if invisible pixies were pulling their eyes and mouths open. "They can't..."

"I thought I'd mark your card, Cath. I mean it might not go through. Although... well... it sounded pretty certain it would."

"It can't be right. It can't be."

"I'm not sure where that leaves you. I suppose you'll be back at your old desk soon. Shall I get IT to get your computer up and running?"

Cathy's nostrils flared with fury.

"Put me through to Stewart, please Mel. Nobody's consigning *my* dream job to history!"

"I can't. He's in a meeting. He'll be another hour."

"Okay... okay... thanks, Mel. Let him know I called, will you?"

"Will do."

Cathy ended the call.

"Everything alright?" said Chris, with possibly a thousand per cent too much fake optimism.

"Unbelievable. Absolutely unbelievable."

"I hope I've got the wrong end of the stick," said Kay.

"They're selling the castle," said Cathy. "Obviously, I wanted to talk to Stewart and possibly put my hands down the phone line to strangle him, but..."

"He's fled the country?"

"He's in a meeting. Now... are you sure this isn't a door into the back of the storage area? It's so full of rubbish, you can't see what's what."

"I think you're in shock," said Chris. "Normally you'd cause a fuss. Like, a really big fuss with casualties."

"I'm fine, Chris. Kay, are you sure about the door?"

"If they sell the castle, what happens to my job?" said Kay, seemingly uninterested in doors.

"Kay, if we overreact to every silly whisper... the door?"

"Well, okay, the storage area wasn't so chock full when I started here. I'm fairly certain there's no door back there."

"Henry might know something," said Cathy, reaching for the office phone.

A moment later, Henry answered.

"Hello?"

"Hi Henry. Cathy here. I'm putting you on speakerphone."

During her first weeks there, Cathy had phoned Henry a number of times concerning various quirks of the castle

— each call being met with more agitation on her predecessor's part. She hardly spoke to him these days, so he was instantly suspicious.

"What's wrong?"

"Nothing's wrong, Henry," said Cathy, waving away Kay and Chris's incredulous looks. "It's about the door behind the bookcase in the office."

"The office door? What's happened to it? It's not the local kids, is it? They'd steal anything."

"The office door's fine, Henry. I'm talking about the door we found when we moved the bookcase in the office."

"You moved the bookcase? What for?"

"That's not important. What's important is we found a hidden door behind it."

"Are you sure?"

"Yes, I'm staring at it as we speak."

"How did it get there?"

"No idea, Henry." *Perhaps the door fairy put it there.* "Did you ever move the bookcase at any point?"

"Move the bookcase? Whatever for?"

"This was your office for thirty-two years."

"Cathy, I never so much as moved the waste paper basket. According to union rules, I was employed as a site manager, not a furniture removals operative."

"No, well, fair enough. So you wouldn't know where we might find a key to it then."

"No... unless it's with the other keys."

"What other keys?"

"I put odd and spare keys in a pot. Not that I was expecting doors to appear out of thin air."

"So where exactly is this pot?" said Cathy, scanning the limits of the office.

"In the storage area."

"The storage area? You mean that rotten place filled, floor to ceiling, back to front, with rubbish."

"It's not rubbish, Cathy. It's things. They might come in useful one day. Like today, for instance. Try the shelf up on the left."

"Okay, Henry. You've been a help. Thanks."

A moment later, in the courtyard, Cathy had the storage area's double doors open to reveal what appeared to be the contents of a junk yard.

"That's the shelf he meant," said Kay, indicating a crammed, warped plank high on the left-side wall.

But Cathy was craning her neck to look over to the right-hand wall near the back.

"I can't see a door," she said. "Although, the junk in the way doesn't exactly help clear up the mystery."

"It's probably best you stick to finding the key then," said Chris.

Cathy huffed – and then attempted to pull a trolley free. It was intertwined with a stepladder, which was, in turn, inextricably linked with a wheelbarrow.

"I might be able to climb to reach it," she said.

"Are you sure that's the sensible thing to do?" said Chris.

"This lot isn't moving an inch," said Cathy prior to climbing up the first two steps of the ladder and then placing her right foot on the upturned wheelbarrow.

It began to move.

"Oh shiiiii...."

The wheelbarrow fell outwards, allowing the stepladder to fall sideways and pitch Cathy off, where she stumbled backwards, fell over the wheelbarrow and landed with a thud at Chris's feet.

"You were saying...?" said Chris, offering a hand.

"I'm just sizing it up before I go in," said Cathy.

She got up, dusted herself down, poked Chris in the ribs, and eyed the junk heap.

"Right..."

She grabbed the ladder, leaned it against the edifice and climbed. Near the top, she stepped across onto a fridge.

"Hand me the ladder, Kay."

Kay passed it up and Cathy laid it across the sea of junk.

"Cath?" said Chris. "You're not related to Indiana Jones, are you?"

Cathy made her way... slowly... slowly... until she reached the end of the ladder. She got onto her haunches to complete the final few feet.

She found the pot.

"I seriously hope this isn't full of spiders."

She peered inside.

"Ooh, promising."

"Keys?" Chris ventured.

"Yep. To save me dropping them, stand back."

Kay and Chris moved aside as Cathy began throwing the keys onto the courtyard flagstones.

"Easy-peasy," she called.

"You've still got to make it back, Cath," said Chris.

"No problarhhhhhh!"

Cathy disappeared into a hole between a cabinet and a folded table.

"You okay?" said Chris, now sounding worried.

"I think I've broken something."

"Leg, arm, neck?" said Chris, sounding even more worried.

"Crockery," said Cathy. "Someone's stored dinner plates in stacks on the floor."

Her head popped up.

"Now – who fancies finding out what's behind the mystery door?"

"Yeah," said Kay.

"Great," said Cathy. "Then once that's done, I'll drive down to London and attack Stewart with a jousting lance."

4

Those Plans You Had...?

Armed with a dozen keys, Cathy was first to the mystery door.

"Hopefully, one of these hasn't sat in a pot for years for no reason whatsoever," she said, trying the first of seven or eight.

"That's a lot of keys," said Chris. "Maybe there are more secret doors to find?"

"I'm sure there aren't," said Kay. "I reckon a couple of those might be for the toilets we haven't used since forever ago."

Cathy tried another key without luck. And then inserted a third.

"Third time lucky?" suggested Kay.

Cathy continued wiggling...

Clink.

"Bingo!"

"What if someone's in there?" said Chris.

Cathy paused then looked to Kay.

"You reckon it's been shut for at least thirty-two years?"

"If Henry didn't know about it – yes."

Chris shrugged. "That still doesn't rule out someone being in there."

Cathy swallowed drily. "Chris, this isn't a horror movie with stupid teenagers about to unleash Satan's hellhounds and destroy half of Leicestershire."

"No, I'll give you that – we're definitely not teenagers."

Cathy pushed the door. It wouldn't budge.

"You want me to kick it?" Chris offered.

"No, I've got this."

Cathy readied herself to apply a shoulder to the situation. Sometimes it was an advantage to be ten pounds overweight.

She hurled herself at the door.

Crack!

It sprang open... and Cathy stumbled through... and clattered into... items... falling around her...

"What the hell...?"

Kay grabbed the office torch from the bookcase. Shining it into the gloom from the doorway, she lit up Cathy, sprawled across a rotten old carpet, surrounded by weapons in a long narrow space that clearly ran behind the storage area.

"Blimey," said Chris. "Guns."

"Rifles," said Kay. "And that looks like a machine gun."

"Who the hell stashed this lot here?" said Cathy.

"What's that sign?" said Chris.

Kay pointed the torch: 'All Weapons Must Be Unloaded Prior To Storage.'

"Ah," said Cathy. "The army had the castle for years.

They must have stored their guns and ammunition in here."

"Only someone kept a few back when they left," said Kay.

"Right," said Cathy, "we need some answers."

Chris frowned. "As to why the door was hidden?"

"No," said Cathy, "as to why some idiot is selling the castle."

"Oh... that."

Cathy made a call. She drummed her fingers on the desk until there was an answer.

"British Heritage. How may I help?"

"Stewart, please. It's Cathy Chappell at De Gaul Castle. And please don't tell me he's in a meeting. I'm fully armed."

"He's in a meeting, Cathy."

"Yes, well, perhaps you'd ask him to call me back. Tell him it won't just be a lance up his left nostril if he tries to avoid me."

Cathy put the phone down.

"Damn..."

Kay peeked inside the carrier bag.

"Cheddar cheese salad baguettes," Chris informed her. "Homemade with style and talent."

"I'd better wash the plague off my hands then," said Cathy, clearly distracted by the call. "What sort of chocolate did you get?"

"I thought we'd start dieting," said Chris.

Cathy tutted and headed for the porta-loos – specifically, the washbasin in the Ladies.

"Yell if Stewart calls," she said.

Cathy didn't want to go back to London. De Gaul Castle was an opportunity to forge a new career, to show off her entrepreneurial flare, and to immerse herself in real history. It was also a chance to avoid another round of IVF in London. She'd lost faith in it, but knew she would try again if there were no excuses in the way. Although, going back to London and the claustrophobic atmosphere caused by three close friends all having babies...

She knew Chris all too well. If he detected the slightest wish to end the painful, upsetting and, up-till-now, futile struggle for a baby, he would tell her to forget IVF. He'd insist they'd be absolutely fine without children. But she knew he wanted to be a dad. Probably as much as she wanted to be a mother.

Chris watched Cathy disappear into the Ladies. He was worried about her.

"I can't believe it," he said.

"That British Heritage would sell the castle?" said Kay.

"No, that Cathy hasn't hurried back to London and hurled herself at Stewart. It's not like her to fail to overreact."

"We're keeping calm," said Kay. "That's the main thing. The last thing we need is..." But the sound of an old diesel vehicle arriving in the car park at the rear of the castle made her pause. "Actually, *that's* the last thing we need. I'd know that racket anywhere."

"Henry?" Chris guessed.

"He wasn't going to miss out on a secret door mystery."

"Hmmm," Chris mused. Having two site managers in the same space usually ended up in an argument. Even though Henry had retired, he still acted as if De Gaul were his castle and that Cathy were some foreign invader.

While Kay got started on her lunch, Chris looked out

at the main gate. How many important visitors had entered through that portal over the long years?

In the year 1154, a messenger hurried in proclaiming the death of King Stephen to knights emerging from the keep. Almost nine centuries later...

...Henry Hume hurried in proclaiming the death of his phone battery to Cathy emerging from the porta-loo.

"Hi Henry," said Kay as the present and former site managers came into the office. "You're looking dapper today."

"Hello, Henry," Chris said to a well-padded man in his late-sixties who had been failing to carry off the mustard corduroy suit look for the whole of the four months Chris had known him. Henry's wild, bacteria-trap beard didn't nudge him any closer to the word 'dapper' either.

Henry grabbed the torch and peered into the unexplained gun room.

"Captain Bats," he said.

"Where?" said Chris, worried they'd missed a whole dead body.

"Captain Rollinson, known as Captain Bats was the Territorial Army Commander here before the Army handed the place over to us. He was a complete nutcase, fixated on an imminent Russian invasion during the whole of the 1960s, 70s and 80s. There were stories about him being ready to fight the invaders should they reach Leicestershire. Dropped dead in the Red Lion just before the official handover. Looks like you've found his answer to Russia's million-strong invasion force."

"Well, we have bigger worries than some nutty captain," said Cathy.

Henry seemed to sneer haughtily. "If you're wondering how to pay for decorating the new wing of your office – not my problem."

"Mine neither," said Cathy. "In fact it's not even a British Heritage problem."

"Oh?" said Henry, his brow furrowing.

"They're selling the castle," said Chris.

Cathy shot him a look that suggested he'd spoiled her moment.

"Cathy has all the info," said Chris, trying to repair the damage.

Henry's gaze fell on his successor.

"What's going on?"

"I had a call from Melanie Sanchez at HQ. I'm waiting for Stewart to get back to me."

"Selling the castle...?"

Chris offered Henry a chair. He looked like he needed it.

"But why?" Henry continued. "Is it even legal?"

"It's not official yet," said Kay. "It might just be one of those office whispers."

"Over my dead body," said Henry, refusing the chair, puffing out his chest, and wobbling a bit. Chris stepped in front of the weapons room, in case the old boy got any ideas.

As Kay got him to sit down, the phone rang. Cathy snatched it up, checked the number and put it on speaker mode.

"Stewart, thanks for getting back to me. I've heard some horrible gossip about us selling De Gaul."

"You must have bloody good ears."

"So it's true?"

"Look, the old place needs a bit more than the sort of TLC we can afford, so we've accepted an offer."

"That's just plain wrong, Stewart," said Henry.

"Is that Henry? Look, it's an offer from someone who can give it the care and attention it deserves."

"You can't sell it," said Henry.

"It's De Gaul Castle, Henry, not the Tower of London."

"Henry's right," said Cathy. "You can't sell De Gaul. It's an outstanding piece of history."

"Cathy, the only thing outstanding is all the repair work we've been putting off for years. The new party has pledged an amount—"

"We'll match any pledge," Cathy interrupted. "We'll double up on our fundraising."

"We'll have a fete," said Henry.

"And a raffle," said Kay.

"And a beer tent," said Chris.

"We'll easily raise the…" Cathy frowned. "How much do we need?"

"Three million pounds," said Stewart.

"What?" Cathy looked crestfallen. She wasn't alone. "Well, obviously that might take a little longer."

Stewart's sigh came down the phone line.

"King Richard the Third has lured most of Castle Hill's tourists to the fine city of Leicester. Selling De Gaul is simply the best way to secure its future."

Cathy looked forlorn. "There could be important people buried at Castle Hill too. Who knows who we might dig up?"

"Why is it a problem, Cathy? You're only there on a temporary contract. We'll soon have you back at your old desk."

"I don't want to come back – *yet*, I mean."

"I don't see what choice you have."

"Let me stay on and tough it out with the new owner. It'll still be open to the public, won't it?"

"Yes, that will be in the final agreement, but…"

"Good, then I'm staying put."

"You can't."

"Why not?"

"Those repairs? The castle's going to close for twelve months. You'll have to come back to London. Assuming you want to keep a job with British Heritage?"

It was now Cathy's turn to need a seat. She chose the edge of the desk, which wobbled worryingly.

"I'll get back to you, Stewart," she said before ending the call and getting back on her feet.

"So what are you going to do?" asked Henry.

"Nothing silly I hope?" Chris added.

"Round up those guns and follow me," said Cathy.

"Sounds a bit drastic," said Kay.

"I'm not having police marching about in my office. We'll lock them in the ante room in the banqueting hall."

Chris was relieved.

"Hi, is now a good time?" It was a short woman in casual wear at the office door.

"Oh, hi Tina. Yes, come in. You know Henry and Kay... and this is my husband, Chris. Chris, this is Tina Hall from the local newspaper. She's come to get details about our summer plans."

"Well, you're certainly going to have plenty to write about," said Chris.

"Absolutely," said Cathy. "We have a full summer season of events lined up. Let's go up to the top of the keep and I'll talk you through it."

Chris didn't understand. Cathy was acting as if nothing had happened. There would be no full summer season of events. The place would be closing down for a whole year and whatever Cathy said she'd have no choice but to return to London.

Wouldn't she?

He left with Henry.

"Need a ride?" Henry asked as they exited through the main arch.

"No, I'll walk, thanks."

"Cathy's a feisty woman," said Henry.

"She certainly is."

"So full of passion for her career."

"Absolutely."

"She's met her opposite in you, Chris. Mr Calm."

"Well, you know what they say – it's the best recipe for a relationship."

"Do they? Interesting. I read recently an imbalance in passion for life objectives is a slippery slope for a relationship."

"Now, steady on, Henry…"

"It was only a magazine article. Probably nonsense. Bye-ee."

Chris watched him head for the car park. Then he set off down the hill telling himself the castle's former site manager was no authority regarding relationships with women. Cathy would navigate her way through these last days in Leicestershire and then make an orderly return to London. Her frustrations would fade and everything would eventually get back to normal.

And yet a little voice was telling him not to be so sure.

5
Still Waters

That afternoon, wrapped up warm and perched on a foldup canvas camping seat, Chris dangled his rod in the still waters of the local canal – an off-shoot of the Grand Union Canal. As a fisherman, he would have preferred wrestling with the moving waters of the river, but, as of two days ago, it was now close season for open waters. He'd just have to work with the serene canal system until deep into June, which he didn't mind at all – between work commissions, of course. He was keen to get a full-time business up and running rather than continuing with the current pattern of not knowing whether next week would be crammed full of work or an entrepreneurial desert.

However, Henry's stupid comment about a magazine article had disturbed his equilibrium. Questions kept popping up in his mind. Are we the solid couple we think? Can one partner be passionate about their career and the other indifferent to theirs without it affecting the relationship?

He thought back to recent dinner parties. Cathy enthusing, himself a passenger. Was that okay for the future? He hoped he wasn't becoming an empty shell. Her passion was a life-force.

Passion...

Coming to Castle Hill had pulled Cathy away from her friends and their partners. But wasn't he glad to be a hundred miles from them too? Hadn't he begun to enjoy the get-togethers a little less because the majority would discuss the ups and downs of running a business in garden design, teaching yoga, and cake-making or being a primary school teacher or working for a firm creating best-selling video games? Hadn't he begun to gravitate to the insurance agent, the local government pension admin assistant, and the driving instructor?

It wasn't that one group did more important work than the other. It was that one group exuded noisy passion for what they did, whereas the other generally grumbled.

Passion...

Chris was passionate about fishing. He'd once tried to write a book on the subject, based on the connection between angler and nature. He recalled firing up the laptop and typing chapter one – not the actual chapter, just those two words. He supposed the idea behind the book was a feeling, an ambience, something very few souls could put into words – an excuse he used for two weeks until Cathy pointed out there were thousands of fishing books not selling any copies on Amazon.

Chris sucked in a lungful of fresh air. It was a beautiful setting, with the canal disappearing deep into the countryside one way, and under an old stone bridge towards the town the other. It felt like he might not see another person for the rest of the day.

While he fished, he thought of Castle Hill, with its modest High Street, three decent pubs, two good restaurants and one fine old church with a war memorial. They had only been there a few months though, so it wasn't as if he was going to miss the place. Would it have been better to have stayed in London?

No.

He was sure about that. When her garden designer friend Cherise announced she was three months pregnant, Cathy wept. Chris knew they were tears of happiness for her friend, but he also knew they were tears of frustration and sadness for herself. He'd held her that evening, reassuring her it wasn't jealousy, but a perfectly justifiable sense of unfairness that had taken hold. She wasn't a bad person, just a person who experienced life denying her what she wanted most while seemingly handing out babies to anyone else on demand. He knew how she felt. Coming to Castle Hill, deep in the middle of Leicestershire, had put them a hundred miles from the army of babies Cathy's friends were currently producing.

He sighed and thought of his own place in the world.

"Hi!"

He looked away from his fishing line to a small group of people coming down the tow-path from the old bridge. Leading them was a middle-aged man with a confident gait and purposeful stride who was seemingly dressed for jogging – Dave Hanley, a detective inspector with the local police who Chris had met a few times socially.

"Hi Dave. I'm not in the way of a murder hunt, am I?"

"No, I'm on leave for two whole weeks, which means putting my feet up with a coffee and a good book... except my daughter had other ideas."

Chris had heard much of Dave's eight-year-old daughter. Now here she was in a thick red jumper and denim dungarees. He hoped she wouldn't be shy about meeting him for the first time.

"You must be Sam," he said.

"We're the Tow-Path Task Force," said Sam. "Canal volunteers," she added as if Chris might be a bit slow on the uptake. "We keep the cut clean and tidy. The cut is another name for a canal. You can join us if you like. Dad said you never catch any fish."

"Hey," Dave protested.

"Well, Sam, it's not just about catching fish," said Chris.

"We're always looking for more volunteers," said a tall woman in her thirties. She was wearing all the right kit: a zipped-up woolly fleece, heavy green cords and hiking boots. "I'm Caroline."

"And I'm Victor James Howard," said a man of at least eighty. "But do call me Vic. Everyone does. We're just here to do a bit of clearance work."

"Nice to meet you all," said Chris, noting that Vic's attire of buttoned-up heavy charcoal duffle coat over light tan chinos and highly polished tan Oxford brogues failed to define a role in the 'here to do a bit of clearance work' claim.

"I was at Stourbridge," said Vic.

"Oh," said Chris. "Nice place, is it?"

"I'll explain another time," said Dave.

Watching them trundle off, Chris found it charmingly odd. Back in London, he knew a couple of environmentalists. They talked about green issues, wore green t-shirts, and liked green Facebook pages. Here, you didn't bother with any of that – you simply pulled on gloves to cut back overgrowth and weeds.

Chris returned his gaze to his float, motionless on the water.

His dad used to take him fishing. They would drive up to Broxbourne in Hertfordshire and spend hours catching small fry.

He glanced at the volunteers making their way along the tow-path and smiled at the image of Sam skipping along so happily. He recalled being her age when he experienced his first ever overnight trip. He and Dad had a small tent and a small burner to cook their fish, or soup if they didn't catch any worthwhile fish, which proved to be the case. He recalled the sun going down, and Dad saying they wouldn't get into the tent until at least midnight. And no sooner he said it, a huge mutant alien wasp came along, making a terrifying buzzing noise. Then another appeared. And another. Dad yelled "hornets!" and they dived into the tent and zipped it up. Chris spent the next hour refusing to come out. His dad died the following summer.

Chris inhaled the atmosphere of a quiet canal in Leicestershire. He always felt close to his dad when he was out by the water.

A narrow boat came along. So slow, so graceful, gliding through still water at two or three miles an hour. Chris wanted one. It wasn't a Leicestershire thing either – he'd thought about boat ownership in London. Of course, the Grand Union Canal linked the two places and the idea of gliding smoothly between London and the rest of the country held a big attraction.

It was a fantasy, of course. London? Leicestershire? It didn't matter what part of the world he was in, his freelance work veered too often between feast and famine to provide a steady income – more a steady headache. Meeting the monthly mortgage repayments had long since become Life's Big Challenge.

Maybe it was just as well he and Cathy couldn't have children. With his prospects, they'd probably end up living in a tent. An old tent. A leaky old tent. Like the one in his mum's loft. The one he was keeping for a repeat performance a generation on, minus the hornets, hopefully.

When Nature was ready to bestow its gift, of course.

6

Connections

Getting ready for bed that night, a frustrated Cathy watched Chris trying to coax their cat out of the bedroom.

"Go to the kitchen, TT. It's a special cat kitchen. Go on, you'll be *really* comfy there."

She smiled but the business with the sale of the castle had upset her. Chris knew a good bedtime remedy for that, thankfully, but tonight she felt nothing could shift her focus from the impending loss of her dream job.

Slipping under the duvet, she wondered. Could she come up with a new plan? Or more to the point – *should* she come up with a new plan? After all, three million pounds guaranteed the castle's future, so any new plan would have to work on the premise that the new owner wouldn't be deterred from spending the money on the castle.

"Why did we get a cat?" Chris complained, having finally managed to shut Truly-Trudy out of the room.

"Because you're a big softy?"

"Possibly, but this door stays shut. I'm not having a cat standing on my head for no reason at three a.m."

She watched Chris change into a scruffy white Simpsons t-shirt and green camouflage shorts that constituted his nightwear. He had a perfectly good pair of blue shorts that matched that top, but he'd worn those the previous night with a green Charlie Brown t-shirt. Chris didn't place much importance in matching nightwear.

She then watched him go through an unexpected squat and stretch exercise regime.

"Been eating too much, have we?" she asked.

"No, a Botox ninja must have snuck up and injected fat into my bum cheeks while I was fishing. Just working it off."

"A likely story."

"Yes, well, it's been a funny old day," he said, giving up on the exercise.

"Yes," said Cathy. "I've hardly stopped laughing since some idiot decided to sell our castle."

"I know."

"I had a brilliant plan in place, Chris."

"I know."

"Now it's all gone."

"I know."

"I can't believe they went behind my back."

"I know."

"Chris, you keep saying I know."

"I know. It might be something to do with you repeating yourself over and over all evening."

"You don't understand. I had a brilliant plan in place."

"I know."

"And they went behind my back."

"How about we change the subject? I mean we could always…"

"I can't think about that, Chris. Not when I'm about to lose my job."

"Cathy, I'm not insensitive."

"Oh, sorry. I thought you meant… so, what did you have in mind?"

"Er… well… um…"

"Oh Chris!" Cathy threw a pillow at him. "I don't need a cuddle, I need a plan. Obviously, I *had* a plan."

"I know."

"A brilliant plan."

"I know."

"And now it's all gone."

"I'm guessing they went behind your back."

Cathy threw the other pillow at him.

While he restored the pillows to the bed, numbers bubbled up in Cathy's head yet again.

"Chris, what restoration work does De Gaul need that would cost three million?"

"The Victorian bit you work in?"

"No, that just needs burning to the ground and having its ashes thrown into a pit – but that can wait. It's not part of the castle that's open to the public."

"Okay, being serious," said Chris, "there's the crack in the arch, the missing part of the keep, the missing curtain wall, the roof in the rear tower, the moonscape car park… which only has slightly more craters in it than the access road, the lack of a proper reception and gift shop area, the lack of proper toilets… and I guess he does have plans for the Victorian bit."

"There must be a Plan B we can come up with."

"I don't follow you."

"If I worked out a way to cover the cost of all that,

then British Heritage wouldn't need to sell."

"It's three million quid, Cath – and the deal's practically signed and sealed."

"But what if I could get a cheaper price on all the work?"

"I don't think paying cash-in-hand to some cowboy builder to mess things up is the right approach. Anyway, you were always bound to return to London at some point. The dream job was temporary, remember?"

"That's not very helpful."

"It was a twelve-month contract, Cath."

"You know full well Plan A plan took all that into account – and that I would work hard to make it permanent."

"Yes, well…"

Cathy's Plan A had involved boosting De Gaul's visitor numbers, thereby alerting British Heritage to her brilliance at the job. This, she knew, would coincide with the upcoming retirement of Pete Williams, a site manager who oversaw the adjoining region. With budgets being tight, it would be the obvious solution – unite the two regions under her stewardship. It was a no-brainer.

Except now, without De Gaul…

"Why the hell did they have to find Richard the bloody Third under a pub car park in Leicester?"

"Yes, we've been over that…"

"And why did they have to rebury him in Leicester Cathedral?"

"He was one of England's most famous kings, Cath. And they didn't have to move him far. The pub was next door to the cathedral. Very handy."

"I don't have anything personal against King Richard, or the people who located his remains, but it hasn't exactly helped De Gaul over the past few years. I mean all the region's tourists are constantly being sucked away from Castle Hill."

"That guy who's retiring," said Chris. "Couldn't you apply for his job?"

"He's not retiring till September. And I don't want to be based at a crumbling 17th Century stately home in another county. The reason I moved to Castle Hill..."

"*We* moved to Castle Hill..."

"The reason *we* moved to Castle Hill is simple. My family very likely once owned De Gaul."

"No, a branch of your family lived up this way a couple of hundred years ago, including in Castle Hill, but they did not build the castle. That tall tale came from your grandad."

"So?"

"Earth calling Cathy. Your grandad used to sell fake Rolex watches down the market."

"Let's not start dissecting grandads, Chris, otherwise we'll get on to a certain old guy in your family who had some very odd views."

"Fair enough."

"Anyway, something's changed. Every time I go up there, I just know my ancestors went in through that arch."

"As tourists, probably."

"No, it's something more. I just know it."

"Are you sure you're not imagining things? I mean I know you really want this."

"It's grown on me, Chris. I haven't implanted it there like some self-hypnotizing nut. I'm sure there's a connection between me and the castle. Grandad says we built it and, who knows, he could be right. After all, *somebody* built it. Why not one of my ancestors?"

"You need evidence, Cath. Nobody's going to

attribute the building of the castle to your family based on a gut feeling."

Cathy didn't like that. She had started researching her family connections to the castle long ago. There was loads of stuff online. Only, none of it linked her directly with De Gaul. Luckily, Jasmine, one of their new Castle Hill friends, had taken up genealogy and was doing a bit of extra research for her. Handily, Jasmine's dearly-departed dad had been a member of the local Parish council, which meant nobody minded Jasmine rooting through their dusty old records. Not that she'd found anything useful yet.

Chris got into bed, causing a mini earthquake.

"Might as well do a spot of reading then," he said, reaching for a dog-eared Stephen King novel on the bedside table.

For Cathy, coming to Leicestershire hadn't only been about the dream job. It was also about finding a role in life. She had been a devoted daughter, but her parents had very recently moved to the Spanish island of Menorca, leaving her without any active engagement. She was totally ready and still waiting to take up the role of being a mother, of course. Only God, the fates, the Universe or whatever had decided otherwise. Luckily, her passion for history saw her do well at the subject during her schooldays, so working for British Heritage and now coming to De Gaul made sense.

"Sorry if I was a bit insensitive there, Cath. I wasn't looking to trample over your dream."

"No, you're right. There's no evidence my family has a connection to the castle."

"You'll still be able to look for links when we're back in London."

"I know, but you've been inside De Gaul enough

times. Don't you ever feel anything?"

"Apart from cold and damp?"

"You know what I mean."

"You know me, Cath. I don't believe in sensing dead ancestors. It's a shame you can't turn up some photos or something. Did Norman knights take selfies?"

"There must be documents somewhere..."

Cathy wondered for the millionth time. Were her ancestors really the original owners? If they weren't – who were they? Where did they come from? What did they do? If only her grandad hadn't told her stories of the family's Norman connection, she might have settled for an ordinary life.

Chris squeezed her hand.

"I know I'm not a Norman knight or anything..."

"I can't think of anything other than this flipping job, Chris."

"Well, I love history as much as anyone..."

"History isn't your subject."

"Yeah, it is."

"Chris, you remember when I asked what you knew of the Jacobites and you described them as orangey sponge biscuits?"

"Okay, fair point."

Cathy returned his hand squeeze. He would probably annoy most women, what with his obsession with sport on TV, his love of spending ages failing to catch fish, and his carefree attitude to worry – he didn't seem to worry about anything! But he was kind and generous, he made her laugh, and he was patient when it mattered most. Quick to smile, slow to frown. That was Chris. Anger was as dormant in him as a dead volcano. And he often seemed at peace with the world.

"Well, I might as well take in a few pages of violent

horror," he said returning to his book.

"Try to refrain from reading out the scary bits," said Cathy, all too aware of Chris's little habit of sharing gruesome goings-on.

"As if I would," he complained half-heartedly.

Cathy's mum had originally thought Chris was too laid back to make a good husband and that Cathy had made a major error in dumping fiancé Giles. But Giles was dull. Yes, he'd been steady, reliable, and earned good money at a big bank in the City, but he talked endlessly about his work rivals, his bedtime requirements came straight from a dodgy internet site, and his bank had a habit of crushing small businesses for being three minutes late with a repayment.

Chris was different. Unfussy and unfazed. And practical too. When her dad sprained an ankle during a stroll through a deserted part of Epping Forest, Chris carried him half a mile to the nearest pub. Dull banker Giles would have stood over her injured dad searching his iPhone for an app that healed people. Even her mum started to see Chris in a new light after that.

"You know the real reason, of course," she said. "Why I don't want to go back..."

"Yes," said Chris without looking up from his book. "I know the real reason."

She didn't want to discuss IVF or the fear of another failure. Chris would say don't go through with it. He'd say it's fine. She knew how much it meant to him though. It was easier if they were a hundred miles from the clinic.

"Castle Hill's not so bad, is it, Chris?"

"I know everything going on in that brain of yours. You're nuts but I love you and will support you, so yes, Castle Hill is fine for as long as you need it to be."

"Chris...?"

Cathy had changed her mind. Tomorrow, she would take on the world. Tonight, she wanted a cuddle after all.

7

Business As Usual

The following morning, Cathy came down to the sound of the Bee Gees on the kitchen radio and Chris singing along with a tomato ketchup bottle microphone. His high falsetto wasn't quite as impressive as Barry Gibb's.

"When's the world tour start?" she asked.

"We kick off in the bathroom this very morning. Just after you go out, in fact. It'll be a medley of our greatest hits. Shavin' Alive, How Deep is Your Bath, You Should Be Flossing…"

"Twit," Cathy muttered with a smile as she checked her look in the hall mirror. With a white blouse, blue silk scarf under a blue blazer bearing a brass British Heritage name badge, and black shoes polished more vigorously than a Rolls-Royce at a Royal wedding, she looked like… like what?

Thankfully, the dark patches under her eyes didn't look too bad thanks to a bit of make-up. Her snuggle with Chris had been fab but once he was asleep, Cathy began a two-hour session of staring at the ceiling and worrying.

She bent down to Truly-Trudy, who was busy grooming having had breakfast.

"Do I look okay, TT?"

"She thinks you look great," said Chris from the kitchen doorway. "Although those are your work clothes. You always go out in them."

"Yes, but I don't always iron them and apply extra make-up."

"No... no, I suppose not. Is Henry coming in? Don't tell me you fancy him. My God, it's the mustard corduroy, isn't it."

"I can't resist him, Chris. I think it's the wildlife in his beard."

Cathy kissed her man... and then entered the kitchen to put the cereal box back in the cupboard and the milk back in the fridge. She glanced out over the small back garden. That would need some TLC come the summer. But what could you do with a rented garden? Probably just mow it and weed it. She wondered about their window boxes back in Finchley. They were like a mini Chelsea Flower Show each summer. She wondered if their tenants were into growing flowers. They never said. Perhaps they would be gone by the summer. Perhaps she and Chris would be back there, watering an abundance of flora. It was funny how life worked out. Well, not funny ha-ha...

"Chris..?"

"Hmmm?"

"Do you ever get the feeling someone else is in control of your life?"

"Yes, but you're a generous leader."

"I'm talking about higher powers."

"Your mother, you mean?"

"I'm being serious. Don't you sometimes wonder if a higher power has a different plan worked out for us?"

"Hey, if this power is about to double my client list, I'm ready for them to assume command."

"I sometimes wonder if someone, somewhere, is living a similar life to me but with it all going right. You know, a proper relationship with their parents, sister, husband..."

"Hey!"

"Maybe they've got lovely children and a career that means something."

Chris's shoulders drooped a little. Then he re-inflated and gave her a hug.

"You've had a bit of an upset with the job, that's all. It's not the end of the world. We'll get through it like we've got through all the other things."

"I bet the other me doesn't have a slice of toast for breakfast," she said into his chest. "I bet she has croissants, smoked kippers and a glass of Bucks Fizz. Beats your oat flakes."

"There's nothing wrong with oat flakes. Good for the waistline."

She put her arms around his waist.

"I know your tricks. As soon as I go to work, you'll be getting the frying pan out."

He pulled away feigning hurt. Then he kissed her and smiled.

"Have a nice day, gorgeous."

Cathy checked the clock, kissed Chris once more, grabbed her bag, and headed for the front door.

"See you later!"

She opened the door to the postman.

"Morning," he said, proffering a letter.

"Thanks," said Cathy, taking it.

A quick glance at the handwriting and foreign stamps told her who and where it was from. She tucked it into her shoulder bag and headed off to face the day.

Halfway up the hill to the castle, Cathy could see Kay at the main gate, opening the doors to another day. Fifteen years ago, Cathy had marched up this very hill in much the same way. It was the summer after her A-levels and she'd been filled with the desire to learn more about Grandad's implausible story. Rather stupidly, she'd come with a boyfriend called Garth who was filled with a different kind of desire. Luckily, the summer festival was enough to distract him.

Henry would have been running the castle back then – not that she recalled him. As a family tree fact-finding mission, the trip proved a failure, but it did spark a deeper interest in the old place. An interest that had only intensified over the years.

That alone had given her a target for her first year – to beat Henry's idea of a festival with something better. She'd spent the past few weeks getting things moving too. No waiting around until the last minute and then making a few quick phone calls. No, she'd been through Henry's contact lists going back five summers leading to firm commitments from a range of people and organizations. Off the back of that, she'd told practically the entire town how the De Gaul Castle Summer Festival would be bigger and better than ever.

She continued up the hill wondering what the day would bring. Would she learn more about the sale? Would the new owner be revealed? Would the ghosts of her ancestors rise up in protest?

The distant town hall clock struck nine as she marched

through the cracked arched entrance.

"Morning," said Kay, who was unlocking the office door. "You look smart. Sleep much?"

"Morning, Kay – no, not much. Mind you, I must have dozed off at one point because I had this horrible dream where British Heritage was selling the castle."

"Strange – I had the same dream."

"The question is what do we do?"

"We should probably carry on as normal," said Kay. "Until we hear more."

Cathy entered the office and picked up the kettle. Kay was right. They were about to enter a busy time – regardless of who owned the castle. The one thing that needed addressing was this daft business of shutting down for a year. As far as Cathy was concerned, that couldn't be allowed to happen.

Just before lunchtime, volunteer Chris was coming up the hill. He paused, as he often did, to take in the view – not so much of the town, but of the river and the canal a little to the west. How many had stood here and taken in that view down the years, he wondered.

Two yards and almost nine centuries away, Hugh de Gaul took in the view. He certainly had a fight on his hands. His loyalty would keep him going, of course. He loved this new land and no traitorous interloper was going to get the better of him without a battle. Could he rely on his brother, Guy, though? Against their enemies, Guy's fears could not be allowed to undermine the de Gauls.

Chris continued up the hill. Cathy certainly had a fight on her hands. Her passion would keep her going, of course. She loved history and no wallet-wielding interloper was going to get the better of her without a battle.

Yes, Cathy and history...

He recalled that first time they met. It was at some posh manor house. He'd been a spare part at a friend's wedding and was looking to get away early. Only he bumped into a wonderful British Heritage woman who had come by to make sure the venue's first-ever party booking was going according to plan. Cathy sometimes wondered if life was throwing out too many obstacles, but, for Chris, sometimes life handed you the jackpot.

Twenty minutes later, he was in the castle courtyard getting a barbecue underway for a party of sixteen. It was one of Cathy's ideas – a mediaeval banquet.

"Just make sure those burgers are well done," she advised. "We don't want more casualties than a civil war siege."

While Chris worked, Cathy watched Kay with the children among the visitors. She was pointing out a few things to them and making them laugh. Cathy laughed too.

"The main part of the castle is called the keep," said Kay. "Does anyone know why it's called that?"

"Is it to keep people out?" asked a small girl.

"Yes, that's right! The keep is where you can keep safe while keeping your enemies outside."

Kay turned to the adults.

"Guy de Gaul was a staunch supporter of Robert, the 2nd Earl of Leicester, but when Robert changed sides in the civil war it gave the de Gauls a problem. I can explain more later."

Kay turned to the children again.

"Right," she said, "who wants to be thrown in the dungeon?"

Cathy busied herself taking a couple of bags of rubbish round to the badly-surfaced, pothole-infested car park, where, in an hour or two, a yellow council truck would lumber up the winding road to the rear of the castle to collect them. She sometimes wondered about Guy de Gaul. It must have been hard being the lone leader, making tough decisions, being steely and resolute 24/7. By comparison, the trials and tribulations of Cathy Chappell seemed trivial.

A moment later, having dumped the bags by the car park gate, she looked out over the distant river, winding its way west towards the more densely populated parts of the English Midlands. Somewhere over there, after the summer, Pete Williams would be retiring.

Did she want to give up on Castle Hill? How could she walk away with her family's links to De Gaul still unproven? She thought back yet again to Grandad telling her about the family being connected.

Family...

She took the letter from her pocket.

Of course, it was Chris's fault that her parents lived so far away. He turned their heads by showing them millions of photos and endless video footage of a little bay on the Spanish island of Menorca. A few villas here, a small hotel there, a couple of bars, a fish restaurant... it had been a lovely holiday, but that was all – until Chris went to great lengths to recommend it to her parents for their next trip abroad. They went there the following year, fell in love with the place, returned three years in a row, scrapped their plans to retire in north London, and, six weeks ago, moved out there permanently. Cathy was furious, She didn't speak to Chris for a whole morning and they didn't… well… not for a few days.

A glint on water caught her eye – the sun reflecting off a Leicestershire river.

"Who needs Menorca," she muttered.

She opened the letter.

> *Dear Cathy*
> *Just a short note as I know how busy you are. Dad's leg is on the mend. No longer blue. More yellow. Who would have thought a jellyfish could do that much harm. I told him his diving days are over but he won't listen. He thinks retirement should be a challenge. I think it's selfish. I certainly have no wish to become a widow when we've barely been in Menorca five minutes. Still, for a few weeks, he'll be strolling about slowly as God intended for a man of 66.*
> *Anyway, I'm very well apart from my stomach. Too much fruit, I think. Jo wrote to say she and Toby are coming over for a week in May. I can hardly wait to see the bump, which will be six months by then. Hopefully, it's okay for her to fly. I'm sure it must be, otherwise she wouldn't qualify for travel insurance.*
> *We miss you and Chris.*
> *Please do write.*
> *Love Mum and Dad*
> *xx*

Cathy folded the letter and put it back in the envelope. She had many thoughts about her parents – but right now the uppermost thought was why the hell couldn't they buy a bloody iPhone and make video call!

But no – she didn't want to hear about Boris, the name Jo had given to the bump.

Cathy sighed. What fun her sister and Toby would be

having involving Boris the bump in all their conversations. It seemed incredible they had only met in October. When Cathy came up to Leicestershire, she didn't even know Jo's boyfriend's name. And yet, by Christmas she must have been blissfully happy enough to not worry about conceiving.

A distant rumble interrupted her thoughts.

"Someone's early."

Although it had yet to come into view, it would be the council truck trundling up the pot-holed approach road well before its normal time. Although, as it got nearer, it didn't sound quite right. If anything, the noise was actually coming from the sky. She looked up and there it was. A black dot against the blue, steadily growing in size.

8

Tyler

Cathy braced herself for witnessing an emergency landing, because the helicopter was too low and too near. Maybe the pilot was ill or needed to get the machine down before the fuel ran out.

While she prayed it didn't crash, particularly into anything Norman, the helicopter came down gradually... gradually... into the middle of the wide coach-turnaround part of the road before the gate.

"What the...?" uttered Cathy.

Without the rotor coming to a stop, a door opened and out popped a blond man wearing a rugby shirt and denim shorts. Apart from the hair, he looked a bit like Chris – although Chris extricating himself from their secondhand Mini never had quite the same James Bond look to it.

"G'day!" he called mover the noise.

Windblown Cathy coughed at the dust and tried to brush her previously pristine blazer. And then a feeling of uncertainty grabbed her. This reject from *Apocalypse Now*...

"Mr Hall?"

As the helicopter took off again, he stopped in front of her and glanced at her name badge.

"We meet again, Cathy. The name's actually Shane Tyler. The whole Mr Hall thing was to keep the press off the scent. I'm the new owner."

"The new owner?"

"It's all but signed and sealed. You don't mind me bowling in for another look around, do you?"

Before she could respond, he was away, hopping over a pothole and heading for the main entrance. Cathy followed and caught up with him as he paused just short of the arch.

"I see the San Andreas Fault's not looking any better," he said, staring up at the crack.

Again, she had no chance to say anything constructive before he strode forward into the courtyard, where he paused again.

"Right, so first things first – that can go, and so can that," he said, indicating the porta-loos, the Victorian debacle known as Cathy's office and the adjoining older bit that housed all their junk.

"It certainly needs a few changes, Mr Hall, but..."

"Shane... Shane Tyler. Actually, what are your plans?"

"My plans for the castle?"

"No, your plans for yourself. You're temporary, right? Are you going back to London?"

"Shane, if you want me to sit down with you and go over my ideas...?"

Shane Tyler moved further into the courtyard with Cathy in tow. Chris looked up from the barbecue on the far side.

"When that Victorian crap has gone," said Shane, "I'll redo that whole section in glass and steel. And we'll knock a doorway through to the car park."

Cathy didn't like Shane Tyler at all. She much preferred it when he was Mr Hall, the man who could help her.

"You can't knock doorways through the castle's fabric."

"I can there. That part of the original wall fell down and was stolen in 1703. It's only low grade brick."

"Even so."

"Don't let me interrupt your day, Cathy. I'm sure you have lots to do. Maybe you can help the guy on burger duty before he poisons all the visitors."

She watched him head for the rear tower, passing Chris with a nod, and entering as if he owned the place.

Kay came over.

"Isn't that Mr Hall?"

"Yes, except he's morphed into Shane Tyler."

"Have I missed something?"

"Only subterfuge and skullduggery, Kay."

"So Mr Hall is now Mr Tyler?"

"Yes, the guy who's buying the place. I think he's looking where he can put in a pool table and slot machines."

Cathy headed back to the office.

"I need to speak to HQ," she said as Kay joined her. "If we're going to fight this, we'll have to think like mediaeval knights. It's a siege situation, Kay."

"Well, not exactly, Cath. The enemy's inside the castle with us."

"Which means he mustn't be allowed to throw us out. If we stay put, we'll have a voice."

"Will we?"

"The main thing is to be vigilant. The enemy could try anything at any time. We don't know how low he'll stoop. Thank God we turned the desk around. At least he won't be able to sneak up behind me."

Just as Cathy reached for the phone, it rang.

She answered it.

"De Gaul Castle, Cathy Chappell, site manager."

"Hello, my name is Alec Baynard. I'm a structural engineer and I've been commissioned to carry out a survey of the castle. Would it be possible to come up today for a look?"

"It would, normally, but..." Cathy glanced out of the window at Chris stoking the barbecue coals. "There's a fire."

"A fire?"

"Yes."

"Is there much damage?"

By the look of that smoke – several burnt sausages.

"I think we'll be okay, but I can't have you running around with all this smoke. Call again next week, by all means."

"Is there someone—"

Cathy ended the call.

"Now to tackle headquarters."

A moment later, she was speaking with Melanie at the British Heritage London office.

"Mel, I just need someone to tell me there's no such castle buyer known as Shane Tyler so I can clamp this nut in irons."

"That's definitely his name, Cathy. I think you're meant to be helpful until you leave."

"Melanie..." Cathy's ire was bubbling up. "Actually, goodbye."

Shane Tyler stepped into the office.

"Was that London?"

"I'd prefer not to be spied on, Mr Tyler, but yes. They didn't sound too happy about you marching around the place."

"They know the score, Cath."

"You can't turn De Gaul into Disneyland."

"I'm not," Tyler protested.

"You have to keep free public access. This is a community resource. There's probably a law against closing it."

"I'll only be shutting it down for a year."

"I know, but we can't allow it."

"I don't think you get a choice. Besides, after the renovation, it'll be open seven days a week from Easter till Halloween as a world class visitor experience. I just need to know your plans. You're welcome to stay on until the close down, of course."

"You can count on it. This place means a lot to me. I have links going back centuries." *Possibly.*

"Hey, so do I. My lot built the place."

Cathy almost gasped.

"Mr Tyler, I'm reliably informed it was my family who founded this castle."

"Reliably informed by who? I've hired a top genealogist to sort it out for me. Actually, it's my fourth genealogist. Finding actual evidence isn't easy, is it. What have you found?"

"That's private."

"Maybe we're related."

"I doubt it. I don't know any Tylers."

"That's not the line that connects me. The thing is to find the details in history."

"Do you know the history of the De Gauls?" asked Kay.

"Only that they disappeared," said Tyler. "I'm assuming you do the long talk with visitors? I think I saw you when I was last here."

"As Mr Hall?"

"Yes, as Mr Hall. Don't worry, I don't need the talk. I know my 12th Century Leicestershire history. Especially around the civil war." He turned to Cathy. "The one that began in 1135."

"I'm well aware of the civil war, Mr Tyler."

"Most people aren't," said Tyler.

Cathy felt her blood rising. "King Stephen's reign came under threat from his cousin, the Empress Matilda in a period we call the Anarchy. It's pretty fundamental to this place."

"It's the reason the castle was built," said Tyler. "And my lot were there. I can't tell you how many times it's played through my mind over the years. 1153… Stephen as good as defeated… 1154… Stephen dies and Matilda's son is crowned Henry the Second of England… rival factions… distrust over who'd supported Stephen or Matilda… payback…"

"You seem a passionate student of history," said Kay.

"Yes, I love the events that went on around my family's story. There's no-one who knows it as well as me."

Cathy suppressed the urge to swear.

Competitive twonk.

"Anyway," said Tyler. "This place will be closed for a year. When it reopens, I'll be hiring. You're welcome to apply for a position."

Before Cathy could protest, Tyler's phone rang.

"Ah, my structural engineer. Excuse me."

Cathy followed him out of the office, where Chris called from his barbecue station.

"Burger anyone?"

Cathy ignored him, instead watching Shane Tyler head for the gate. She felt a chill but it wasn't the breeze coming down from the north.

"I can feel my ancestors around me," she said to no-one in particular. "They built this castle and I will defend it from marauders and bored rich twits."

Kay came over. Tyler was now outside the main gate, still talking on the phone.

"Kay, we're going to war against Shane Tyler."

"We?"

"I can't do it alone."

"Okay, but why exactly? He's going to pay for the repairs this place needs."

"That's a side question, Kay – and I will provide an answer in due course. Right now though, my blood is up and we need some action."

"What kind of action?"

Cathy considered it.

"Good question."

9

Family Trees

On the Saturday evening, just after six-thirty, Chris was in the bedroom getting ready for a party a few doors down in Castle Close. He eyed Truly-Trudy, who was sprawled across the duvet with no hint of moving anytime soon.

"Lucky cat. You get to stay in and watch the Bond movie on TV. Octopussy, in fact."

It wasn't a party he was particularly looking forward to. Grace Darling's 82nd birthday was likely to be cups of tea and sponge cake. Not Chris's idea of a Saturday night.

He splashed a little Hugo Boss aftershave around the gills and peered out of the window. At the top of the street, where it joined the main road, a woman with a baby's pushchair was crossing.

"I won't be long," Cathy called from the bathroom. "Unless you need the loo?"

"I'm fine," he called back.

Not that Chris didn't like Grace – far from it. She was a feisty free spirit who had welcomed them to Castle

Close right from the start.

He checked his look in the small mirror. No good. You needed the big mirror in the hall downstairs to get a proper look. Luckily, men like Chris knew instinctively that a rugby shirt, comfy jeans, and slip-on tan loafers always looked good. Plus, it only took forty-five seconds to get ready.

"You're not wearing a rugby shirt and jeans, are you?"

At the top of the stairs, Chris wondered why Cathy felt the need to hurl random questions from the other side of the bathroom door. For all she knew, he was standing there in a pinstripe suit with a frilly shirt.

"What's that, Cath?" he said, heading downstairs. "I couldn't quite hear you over the rustling of my silk cravat."

It had been a strange week. After all the fuss created by Shane Tyler's flying visit, everything had gone quiet – as if it had never happened and they were free to continue with their lives as planned. Tyler was apparently in London now, running his other business interests and nobody knew when he'd be returning to Castle Hill.

Of course, it was merely the calm before a storm of Tyler's making – one that would probably wash them away.

As it was, the storm front wouldn't arrive until British Heritage put it on their website. Their notice to members would give details of the new arrangements at De Gaul and hail Mr Tyler as a rescuer. Of course, he would be tied to various agreements and limitations. After that, it would be up to Cathy to decide what she wanted to do. Go back to London or hang around under Tyler until closedown, which would probably be in a couple of weeks' time – when Tyler's hired specialists would have finished their current project in York and arrived in

Castle Hill.

Cathy had expressed her views in no uncertain terms: "I'm staying and I'm fighting."

But fighting what? She'd have to return to the British Heritage office in London or lose her job.

As far as Chris could see, Cathy had zero chance of raising three million, meaning her new plan had to revolve around persuading or possibly blackmailing Shane Tyler to keep the castle open the whole time, with work on the various parts to be undertaken in separate stages. That would leave Cathy's original plan intact – to stay on as site manager *and* take over responsibility for the adjoining region when Pete Williams retired in September. Except the second part of the plan would require Tyler to agree to British Heritage running his prized possession, which he had yet to indicate was likely.

Grace welcomed Cathy and Chris into her home with a hug. Chris was slightly taken aback by her 1960s floral kaftan that might have doubled as a bedspread, but said nothing on account of his firm belief that people should wear what made them comfortable.

"Thanks for coming, you two," said Grace. "I thought we might hit a nightclub later, but then I realized you're probably a bit old for that kind of thing."

"Is that Elvis I can hear?" said Chris, suddenly pulling a quick dance move – too quick, as he almost pulled a hamstring too. Cathy simply handed over flowers, a card and a bottle of Cabernet Sauvignon.

Grace thanked Cathy then turned to Chris. "No getting drunk and throwing yourself at me, okay? At least not while Cathy's in the room."

They were shown into the front half of a tastefully

decorated through-lounge, which was separated from the back half by lightly frosted glass doors. Kay was already there, perched on the sofa, glass of wine in hand, tapping her foot to the rock and roll soundtrack.

"Tell me about the castle," said Grace. "Is there any more news?"

"I've been keeping Grace up-to-date," said Kay, "but she obviously requires a minute-by-minute news feed."

"There's nothing more than you've seen or heard, Grace," said Cathy. "There'll be an official announcement soon-ish. Hopefully, it'll say Shane Tyler has changed his mind and pulled out."

"We don't really want that," said Grace. "It's only right someone spends some money on the old place."

"You're right, Grace. I'm overreacting. But there's no need to close it down for a year."

"We don't know that for sure, Cath," said Chris. "It could be dangerous with all that work going on."

"We've been told to stop taking bookings," Cathy told Grace, ignoring her husband. "We'll still be doing the fireworks, though. He's agreed to allow that."

"There's a ton of other commitments we'll have to bail out on though," said Kay.

"That's what annoys me," said Cathy. "What about the big summer festival we planned? I've given people my word."

"Ah well," said Grace, "at least it was only a temporary job."

"As you know, I had a plan to change that. Temporary wasn't going to mean temporary."

"But it does now," said Chris.

The doorbell rang. Jasmine and Roland had arrived.

Blonde Jasmine's tight red jumper and even tighter black leggings made Chris look quickly to Roland, who seemed dressed for a business meeting.

Jasmine held out a bottle of Sauvignon Blanc.

"It's organic," she announced as if to calm any anxieties on that score.

While they settled down with drinks and began a leisurely study of a Chinese takeaway menu, the conversation turned again to the castle.

"I'm hearing Shane Tyler is convinced his family built De Gaul," said Grace. "No proof though. A bit like Cathy."

Chris nodded. "I'm just waiting for Cathy to start digging up bodies and going for a DNA match."

"Now there's an idea," said Cathy. "Anyone know where they're buried?"

"They found Richard the Third behind a pub," said Kay, "so we'll probably find some knights under Jasper's Wine Bar."

"It's just a matter of finding a link," said Cathy. "That's all."

Grace shook her head. "My dad spent a lifetime trying to prove our family's link to the castle. He never succeeded."

"Oh well," said Kay. "Maybe it wasn't meant to be."

"Maybe Jasmine's going to change my luck," said Grace.

"Oh?" said Cathy.

"She's helping me with a bit of research," said Grace.

"Me too," said Cathy. "Although I didn't know she'd be working for a rival."

"I'm a professional," said Jasmine. "Any information will remain confidential."

"Shane Tyler reckons he's hired a genealogist too," said Chris. "I'm beginning to feel left out."

"I feel sorry for anyone working for Tyler," said

Cathy. "It must be some desperate amateur he's teamed up with."

Jasmine coughed a little. "Um…"

Chris felt the penny drop with a clang.

"Yes, a top, top genealogist," he said, giving Cathy the eyes.

Cathy sighed. "Jasmine, how could you?"

"Lots of reasons, Cath."

"Name one."

"He's paying me."

"Ah."

"You and Grace are my freebies – which is fine. I'm building up a business and it's good to help friends in the early days."

"So what have you learned about Tyler?"

"Cathy, please, it's confidential."

"Jasmine, come on – you said yourself we're friends."

"Okay, so he's told a few people his ancestor Jeremiah Dupris inherited the castle from an unknown relative in the 1670s. He says Jeremiah is the descendent of the family who built the castle."

"What a load of rubbish," said Grace.

"Maybe," said Jasmine, "but he's hired me to find evidence."

Cathy snorted. "How could a show-off dipstick like him have links to De Gaul?"

"It makes sense," said Roland. "Many of the knights who flourished in those times would have been show-off dipsticks."

"Wouldn't the Land Registry have all the details of who owned the castle?" asked Chris.

"The Land Registry isn't as old as you might think," said Jasmine. "It only came in around the 1860s… 1862, I think. Prior to that, all records were held locally."

"And we're missing many of ours," said Grace.

"Was it the Dupris family who sold the castle to the army?" said Chris.

"Indirectly, yes," said Jasmine. "Tyler's great grandfather Harold Dupris had significant tax debts, so the State acquired the castle as part of the settlement. Then, with the Second World War looming, it was handed over to the army as a training base."

"British Heritage took it off the army in 1982," said Cathy.

Chris thought about his own family line. His great-grandad was a dock worker; Grandad, a road-sweeper; Dad, a van driver. Chris himself was a web designer-copywriter, and, going forward… the next generation looked like it might remain an unwritten story.

Not wishing to contribute to the debate, he studied the divider doors. The frosted glass had clear swirls in the pattern.

He peered through.

"Hello…?" he uttered.

While Cathy, Jasmine and Roland discussed dipstick knights, Chris caught Grace's attention and indicated what he'd seen. Grace came over and opened the doors for him.

Chris turned to the company.

"Before you lot launch into a feudal war, you need to see this."

Cathy, being closest, was first.

"Good grief."

All were soon gathered in the back half of the lounge.

"It's like the crime boards you get in cop shows," said Kay.

There were two white boards, in fact – both plastered with old photos, maps, newspaper cuttings. These exhibits had comments written below them in black marker. Some also had arrows running from one exhibit to another. And there was a family tree.

Chris moved in closer.

"You see this, Cath? Grace's line goes back... a long way."

"Not far enough yet," said Grace. "I'll get there though."

Cathy turned to Jasmine.

"You didn't know about this?"

"Yes, but's it's... *was* confidential."

"I did it all," said Grace. "I'm hoping Jasmine can prove or disprove some of it."

"Well, Cathy's made some progress too," said Chris. He turned to his wife. "Your great uncle was a butcher in Leeds. Isn't that right?"

Cathy huffed. "Maybe we should get Tyler over," she said. "We could compare what we know."

"I don't think he's the collaborative type," said Jasmine. "When I told him I was doing a bit of work for you and Grace, he wasn't impressed."

"You told him?"

"He's the only one paying me, remember? Anyway, he made it clear he'd be happy if I found anything that discredited you both."

Cathy was annoyed. "First he takes my job away, now he's trying to chop down my family tree."

"He's not linked to the building of the castle," said Grace.

"There's no proof either way," said Jasmine.

"Well, which of you is it then?" said Chris. "Who built the old place?"

"Don't you worry about that," said Cathy. "We'll get to the bottom of it eventually."

"How?" said Chris.
But his question just hung there.

10

Down by the Canal

The Sunday lunchtime sunshine felt warm on Chris's back. He'd been dangling a line into the canal for an hour without success, but that was just fine. Besides, it was time for his giant cheddar cheese and mango pickle sandwich.

His first bite coincided with him catching sight of a narrow boat coming in from the countryside. He'd got a fair way through the sandwich by the time it was passing him. He nodded to the middle-aged couple at the wheel.

What a wonderful way to spend the day.

He also noted the tastefully painted cabin. Against a black background were castles surrounded by roses. He'd noticed that a lot – narrow boats decorated by genuine artists. No slapping on a coat of green gloss and saying 'job done'.

He watched it pass under the old bridge on its way through the town. Above it, leaning on the stonework, peering down into the water, was a casually dressed man in his late-thirties.

Shane Tyler.

Obviously back from his business activities in London. He noticed Chris looking up.

"G'day," he called.

"You're the bloke who's buying the castle then," Chris called back.

"That's me."

"I'm Chris. Why don't you pop down and say hello?"

Shane Tyler was soon standing alongside the seated Chris on the tow-path. With both in rugby tops and jeans, they might have been brothers.

"Good to meet you properly, Chris. Last time I saw you, you were busy flipping burgers."

"I sometimes volunteer to help out."

"Good man. You caught anything yet?"

"Not yet." Chris put the remainder of his sandwich back in his lunchbox. "So you were here as Mr Hall and now you're back as Shane Tyler."

"I needed to check it out first. Now I'm back to take a more hands-on approach. Do you know the crazy woman who's running it?"

"Er…"

"Just kidding. I'm guessing Cathy's your missus. A feisty one, she is."

"That's Cathy."

"I like her. I respect her views, too. It's just that once we get started we won't be hanging back. Have you seen the crack in the arch?"

"It's hard to miss."

"I texted Cathy about it. She texted back, practically accusing me of trying to buy my way into history."

"We're talking about her dream job, Shane – except it's now pretty much over."

"It doesn't have to be. I've already said we'll be hiring next year."

"We'll be settled back in London by then. I'm not sure we'll be tempted away a second time."

"Fair enough. I don't usually go out of my way to spoil things for people."

"So, your family built the castle?"

"That's right, Chris. Not far off nine hundred years ago. It really drives me on, mate. Know what I mean?"

"I guess so…"

"Family connections. Heritage…"

"Yeah, so what would happen if you found out you weren't connected to the people who built it?"

"That just flies in the face of the known facts."

"I didn't think there *were* any known facts."

"I know all the facts, Chris. I'm just waiting to confirm them."

"Best of luck then. Personally, I'm trying to keep out of it. Mind you, I don't think I'd be too bothered about spending millions on an old pile if it didn't have my DNA running through it."

"You're right there, Chris. Good luck with the fishing, mate."

Chris watched him go and then rescued his sandwich. He and Cathy couldn't stay on in Castle Hill once the castle was closed for repairs. Cathy would have to swallow her pride and get back to the office in London. Yes, she'd hate it for a bit, but she'd get used to it again. And at least she'd have the bonus of being able to look back on a lovely few months living the dream at De Gaul Castle. She'd settle for that, wouldn't she?

He checked his phone. No messages. He then googled rental accommodation in north London – after all, they had tenants in their place in Finchley on a twelve-month arrangement and it wouldn't be right to try to dislodge them early.

An hour later, packing his stuff away, Chris spotted a familiar group farther out along the tow-path. They appeared to working their way towards him, clearing an overgrown stretch.

Dave came over.

"Good session, Chris?"

"In terms of relaxation, yes."

"It's good to get away from work every now and again. I guess your business keep you busy?"

"Yes… mainly. I'm working for a client who imports low cost clothing from the Far East. Writing copy for his website, kind of thing. Not as hectic as working for the police, I'd imagine."

"It certainly never stops, Chris. This is the first break I've had in ages, but I still had to assist with a case against a conman who's been preying on the elderly. The crazy thing is I can't wait to get back to work. It's what I do."

"Same here," said Chris, unconvincingly. But surely it was okay to build a business you had no interest in. Dave might be as dedicated to police work as Cathy was to history, but someone had to assist the guy selling dirt cheap clothing from developing countries.

"Fancy volunteering?" Dave asked.

"Oh… um…"

But Chris didn't like to be endlessly negative with those who made the canal a nice place.

"I can spare an hour if that's any use."

"Perfect," said Dave. "I'll put you in the hands of our top Tow-Path Taskforce instructor."

Chris looked along the tow-path to Caroline, but it

was Dave's young daughter, Sam, who was summoned.

"We have a new volunteer, Sam. Could you do your checks, please?"

Chris felt a bit of a twit, but said nothing.

"I just have to check you for sensible clothing," said Sam with great purpose. "Sensible shoes, check. Jeans, check. Very old sweat shirt, check."

Bloody cheek.

"Our tasks change all the time," Sam continued, "but over the next few months we'll be lock-painting, hedge-planting, weeding, clearing litter from the water and anywhere else we find it, and making some tow-path repairs."

"Thanks, Sam, I think I'll remember all that."

He didn't like to mention he wouldn't be in Castle Hill much longer.

"This way then," she said, marching off.

"Oh... right."

"See you in a bit," said Dave.

Clutching his fishing bag and rod, Chris felt like an oversized new kid in school as he followed Sam. They headed away from the town, a good hundred yards, before turning left where an arm off the main canal headed towards a derelict area. They only got a hundred feet into this narrow stretch of water before it reached a set of decrepit lock gates. The lock chamber beyond was empty apart from a muddy sludge puddle, and the gates at the other end seemed to be there solely to hold back a forest. It was here they found Vic and a middle-aged volunteer called Liz at work.

Once Sam had got them up to speed on Chris's intention to help, Liz produced a hi-viz tabard from a sports bag and handed it over.

"This is the old industrial arm of the canal," said Sam.

"It's a bit short," said Chris, dumping his gear and taking the tabard.

"It wasn't always so," said Vic. "It used to run beyond this lock half a mile down to four factories. Of course, it's been through all the phases since it was a busy stretch of water. By that I mean declining, silting up, dead dogs and supermarket trolleys, and now forest."

"Right," said Chris. "It's a deforestation job then, is it?"

Liz issued him with secateurs and a pick-axe. Chris had to bite his tongue while Sam explained how to use them.

Fully apprised of all issues, including health and safety, Chris was soon hacking, cutting and pulling up the woody vegetation that had been taking root for decades.

"Keep that up, Chris, and you might find the lost pub," said Sam.

Chris looked up. "Lost pub? You make it sound like an Indiana Jones movie."

"No, it's only a pub," said Sam.

"Right."

"And it's lost," said Liz.

"How can it be lost? Did it wander off in the night?"

Sam chuckled. "It's not really lost."

"It's fifty yards through there," said Vic, "which, as I pointed out, used to be clear and open water."

Chris tried to picture it. "You mean you could be in your boat and turn in here… through the lock… and pull up beside a pub? What a brilliant concept."

"You could still do it," said Vic. "If you restored the cut and renewed the lock gates."

Chris tried to see through the woods, but it was too dense. Still, he would put that on his list of things to do before he and Cathy left Castle Hill for good: Find the lost pub.

"Do you like fishing a lot?" Sam asked.

"Yes, ever since my dad started taking me when I was your age."

"What bait do you use?"

"Wriggly maggots."

"There's a lot of advice online about how to catch fish in the canal."

"Yes, I expect there is. I *do* catch fish, you know."

"If you examine my statement forensically," said the eight-year-old daughter of a detective inspector, "you'll see I never said you didn't."

Chris smiled. Sam was an intelligent kid.

"Let's carry on hacking this never-ending patch of bramble," he said. "Then we can have a crack at that patch of never-ending buddleia."

He stepped farther forward and dropped a good twelve inches into boggy mud.

"It's probably best if you stay in sight of everyone," said Sam. "You'll be safer."

Chris extricated himself and found firmer ground. Once he was able to restart his work, he found himself with Vic, who seemed keen to talk.

"Do you know the first canal in Britain?"

"Um… no. I could google it, if you like?"

"Bridgewater," said Vic, who, as far as Chris was concerned, looked worryingly set for a lecture. "In 1761, the third Duke of Bridgewater wanted a reliable way to transport his coal to the factories in Manchester – so he commissioned the engineer James Brindley to build a canal."

"Right. Interesting."

Chris tried to get back to work, but Vic wasn't so easy to shake off.

"By the 1830s, Chris," he continued, "there were enough canals to create a network that connected the whole of England. All built by hand. *By hand*. Think about that for a minute."

"Hard work," said Chris. "Just trying to clear this lot is already doing my back in."

"These canals were the lifeblood of the Industrial Revolution."

"I can imagine."

"Horses!"

"Where?" Chris looked around.

"A single horse can only pull a small loaded cart," said Vic. "But you put that horse on the tow-path, fix a rope to a narrow boat, and there you go. That one horse is now pulling forty tons."

"That's impressive, Vic. Anyway, I'd better get on…"

"Narrow Boat."

Chris looked back at the main canal for one – but the waterway was clear.

"Narrow Boat," said Vic. "The book by Tom Rolt."

"Oh right."

"I don't mean any book, Chris. I mean *the* book. The one that changed everything. The one that saved all this from destruction."

Chris looked around.

"What, one book saved this bit of canal? It looks pretty neglected to me."

"No, son, Tom Rolt's book saved all the canals in the whole of Britain, for everyone, for all time."

"Right, well… that's incredible. One book, you say?"

"Narrow Boat by Tom Rolt."

"Maybe I'll get Cathy to buy me a copy for Christmas."

"It's a wonderful tale, Chris. Just as the Second World

War was brewing…"

"Now, no spoilers, Vic – and I really ought to be getting on…"

"…Tom Rolt and his wife Angela took the narrow boat Cressy on a wonderful four hundred mile journey along the canals of the Midlands. They turned Cressy into a home and met all kinds of boat people along the way."

"I really will buy a copy. Promise."

"It's an elegy, Chris. A lament for a world lost to us."

Chris sensed sorrow in Vic. But times change. Things move on to the next phase. Wonderful stuff gets left behind and forgotten. It was the way of the world.

But Vic wasn't finished.

"Do you know how the public greeted that book when it was published at the end of the War?"

"No…?"

"They couldn't get enough, Chris. It was the greatest enthusiasm from a people tired of death and destruction. Do you know that single book led to the formation of the Inland Waterways Association?"

"No, I didn't."

"Oh yes. Like I said, that one book led to the rescue of our canals from the mindless lunatics in government who wanted to shut them all down and fill them with concrete."

"Well, in the spirit of that book, it certainly has to be worth clearing this lot and getting those lock gates working," said Chris.

"An expensive business," said Vic. "A *very* expensive business."

Chris thought about that. Wasn't there someone in their midst who might have the money to pay for a clean-up and restoration job? Assuming Cathy didn't chase him off from De Gaul Castle first?

But then Chris retired the thought. He wouldn't be in Castle Hill for much longer. There really was no point in him getting involved in canal restoration. Was there?

He got back to work, and even managed to shake off Vic. And while he uprooted and cut down, he pondered the idea of finding a passion he could turn into a career. He imagined Cathy being pleased with a re-energized husband who would enthrall people with his tales. Then it came to him.

Collectibles.

He could buy and sell old toy cars on eBay. Why hadn't he thought of that before?

11

Knowledge is Power

While Chris was enjoying some Sunday downtime on the canal, Cathy was at home checking a genealogy website on her laptop. Despite having half the keyboard obscured by a cat, she was studying the Barrett line – a branch of the family on her mother's side living in the Midlands in Victorian times.

According to the 1861 census, nineteen-year-old sawmill worker Frederick Barrett was residing in Amble Street, Castle Hill. Of course, Cathy had come across him before, but had yet to find any trace of him prior to this date. Certainly the 1851 census had nothing to say about him as a nine-year-old and during the 1841 census Frederick would have been no more than someone his parents were actively trying to create.

Cathy nudged Truly-Trudy aside and got up to stretch. Their stomachs rumbled in unison.

While wondering what to do about lunch, Cathy went to the back window. Not for the first time, she wondered

– come the summer, what blooms would they see in their rented garden? Or would they be back in London before then?

She was annoyed that the summer festival might not go ahead. She wouldn't close the door on the possibility of doing something though. She had stayed in touch with all the committed parties – and they had yet to learn of Shane Tyler. Perhaps she would find a date in the next couple of weeks and ask them to keep it free in case some overbearing ass went through with a plan to close the castle.

She went to her handbag on the worktop by the fridge. Tucked inside was the latest letter from the IVF clinic. She didn't want to go back to London for another round of treatment. She feared another emotional rollercoaster ride all the way to the usual destination. Of course, she knew what Chris would say if…

The doorbell rang. A moment later, Cathy was greeting a familiar face.

"What are you doing for lunch?" said Kay.

"Er… cat food and toast?"

Kay tutted. "I saw Chris go out with his rod earlier. He's probably in the pub by now."

Cathy almost laughed. "No, if Chris says he's going fishing, there's nothing short of an alien abduction that would stop him."

"Good, then he won't see us in there then."

"Oh… not sure."

"Wait, I haven't sold it to you yet. The Albion does lightly spiced chicken breast, a wedge of hot garlic bread, a small mixed Mediterranean salad, and a glass of Prosecco – all for a tenner."

"Sold. Come in, I'll just sort out TT with a tin of something."

*

An hour later, having finished their pub lunch, Cathy and Kay were enjoying an 'oh, go on then' chocolate mousse dessert and second glass of Prosecco.

"I just don't trust him," said Cathy of Shane Tyler, not for the first time.

"You're right," said Kay. "How best to sum him up? Impossible to trust, but possible to fancy?"

Cathy almost spluttered on her dessert. "What?"

"I'm just saying – he's quite fanciable in some ways."

"Kay, sometimes we have to look beyond the money and the helicopter."

"Do we?"

"You can do better than Shane Tyler, Kay."

"Really? You wouldn't know when the other guy's beat-up old car is due in town, would you?"

Cathy could see she was trespassing.

"Sorry, Kay – I wasn't trying to run your life for you."

"There's nothing wrong with having a rich boyfriend."

"Agreed. I just don't trust him with the castle, so I'm not likely to trust him with a good friend either."

"Well, if I'm being honest, he's not my type. I just thought it might be an interesting experiment to have tens of thousands of pounds lavished on me – per day."

Cathy laughed, but then sighed.

"The truth is I don't want to go back to London – which means I have to stay and fight Shane Tyler."

"I know, but people often say things when they're frustrated. I can't see how you can fight him, or why you'd want to. You love the castle as much as anyone."

"I know it needs big money spent on it, but I don't see why it should close down for a year. That's just Tyler not caring about the public."

Kay drained her glass.

"It's true I'd prefer to work there while the improvements get under way," she said. "As it stands, I'll have to get a job in a pub or something."

"That's another reason it shouldn't close. If we could persuade him to keep it open, I could stay on and unite the two regions when Pete Williams retires. If I'm in London, I just have this feeling I'll never get back here."

"Sounds like we need a plan then," said Kay, "and possibly more Prosecco."

After lunch, Cathy and Kay went their separate ways, as Kay wanted to pop along to see her parents. Cathy meanwhile headed back towards Castle Close.

She hadn't got more than twenty yards when, just ahead, Shane Tyler stepped out of a big black car with tinted windows. He was in the middle of a phone call.

Cathy ducked into a shop doorway and listened. It seemed to be a call relating to the castle and money.

Annoyingly, Tyler took a few steps away, making it harder to hear him. Luckily, the three glasses of Prosecco coursing through Cathy's veins told her it was okay to sneak up much closer... even to the rear of the vehicle he was now alongside. And when the vehicle's owner got in and drove off, leaving Cathy in plain sight on her knees in the road, the clever Prosecco told her to pretend to be looking for a missing earring.

That afternoon, Cathy shared the sofa with Chris and Truly-Trudy in front of a spy film that only Chris was watching. At least she thought he was watching it. He seemed more engrossed with his laptop.

"Work?" she asked.

"Passion," he said.

"Oh God, not some lurid website."

He showed her what was occupying him. To Cathy it looked like toys on eBay.

"My new business venture," he said. "Like you, I'll be merging my passion with my profession, thereby making myself even more desirable."

"What are you talking about?"

"Buying and selling toy cars."

"Chris, what are you doing? You know we never buy children's toys. It tempts Fate against us."

"They're not *toy* toys, they're collectible toys. Twenty years from now this one's value will have doubled."

"Have you bought it?"

"Of course I have. That's the whole point."

"How much did you pay?"

"Five dollars plus postage. It was a guy in Florida selling it."

"Well, we can sit back and wait ten years for that to roll over to ten bucks. With a bit of luck, taking the postage into account, you might break even."

Chris closed the laptop and started watching the movie.

Cathy sighed. She hadn't intended to irritate her partner.

"Did I mention that stupid ancestor of mine is still a dead end?" she said just as a bad guy was sneaking up on the good guy.

"Hmm?"

"The ancestor I was looking up in the 1861 census. Nineteen-year-old sawmill worker Frederick Barrett."

"Oh right."

"He lived in Amble Street, Castle Hill, but prior to that

he was being held captive on Mars by aliens."

"Right."

"Obviously that's not recorded in the 1851 census."

"Right."

"The census didn't cover Mars back then."

"Mmm."

"Chris!"

"What?"

"I was saying I couldn't find Frederick Barrett in the 1851 census."

"Oh right. Bad luck."

"I just wish I could find something to back up grandad's story."

"Never gonna happen, Cath. Besides, Tyler's taking over now. It's game over."

"This isn't about avoiding going back to London, Chris."

"I never thought otherwise."

"I'd just love to prove my family built the castle."

"But you don't actually believe that, Cath. It's one of your grandad's tall stories."

"It could be true. He always gets very animated when he talks about it."

"He gets very animated when he talks about anything, Cath. Usually because he's got a drink in his hand. Tell you what – why not call him in the morning when he's sober. If you push him, he might give you a different version of the castle story."

"That's not very supportive."

"No, you're right. Sorry. Oh, on another matter – I found a couple of flats for rent in Finchley."

"Why? We're not going back yet."

"I know, but we'll need to set things up in advance."

"We don't know if I'll lose the castle job yet."

"Yes, we do, Cath. Shane Tyler said so."

"Yes, but I'm going to make him see sense."

"How?"

"Whose side are you on?"

"Yours, of course."

"This is serious. We didn't come to Leicestershire for a long weekend. I had sleepless nights for months plotting and planning this. Then I had all the fears and concerns it might go wrong. Then you put me under pressure saying we'd return to London if it didn't work out. I had to work hard on myself to go for it."

"I know, Cath, I know."

"I don't want to live in temporary accommodation in Finchley. I want to stay here and fight."

"Okay, I understand – but how do you plan to make Tyler see sense?"

"I was thinking… what if I had public opinion on my side?"

"I don't understand."

"What if I rallied the town to my cause?"

"It's Tyler's castle, Cath."

"So?"

"So, the one thing he's said he'll do is spend millions on it. How the hell are you going to rally the town against that?"

Cathy didn't say.

Chris put an arm around her. He knew she was happy in Castle Hill, away from friends with babies and the endless discussions that revolved around having little bundles of joy. This was the life she needed and it was being taken away from her.

"How about we spend Sunday afternoon in a different location?" he suggested. "One about ten feet above this one? That's the bedroom, by the way – saves you trying to work it out."

"I did think about getting a job outside of history, but that just made me annoyed. Why should I start working outside of the one thing I've been inside since school?"

"You've had spells outside of it. When we met, you were in events management."

"Events management for British Heritage, Chris."

"True…"

"I'll tell you one thing. I can't have him knowing more about 12th Century England than me. Have you heard him? He sounds like he's swallowed a cheat sheet."

"I'm sure he doesn't know half of what you do, Cath."

"No, he doesn't."

"So… er… upstairs?"

"Let's play a little game."

"Now you're talking."

"I mean a quiz."

"What?"

"Test me on Stephen and Matilda."

"The couple who run the bakery?"

"Stefan and Marta run the bakery. I'm talking about King Stephen and the Empress Matilda. Ask me any question you like."

"How's that meant to get us in the mood?"

"Tyler's trying to give the impression he knows more than me."

"It's not a competition, Cath."

"Yes, it is."

"Okay, it's a competition then… and the results are in. Tyler wins by three million quid."

"Christopher…"

"Okay, okay."

"The quiz."

"Right… um… what did Stephen and Matilda get up

to?"

"Too easy. Ask me about the man Guy de Gaul supported... Robert, the 2nd Earl of Leicester. No, ask me about Robert's support for King Stephen."

"Consider it asked."

"You're being very generous using the word 'support', Chris. He spent most of that period fighting a private war with the Earl of Chester."

"Of course he did. How stupid of me."

"Yes, but Robert wasn't daft. As soon as he'd won strategic parts of Chester, he immediately brought all the earls of England together to seek peace in all areas."

"He sounds like your mum when we played cards last summer. As soon as she went a fiver up on me she said 'game over' and stuffed the money in her purse."

"The year before Henry II was crowned, Earl Robert sensed which way the wind was blowing, met him in secret, and agreed to change sides from Stephen to Matilda, Henry's mother."

"Right, well, that's definitely put me in the mood, Cath. How about you?"

"Robert promised to support Henry, partly in return for being appointed Justiciar of England."

"Just-what?"

"It's like the Prime Minister. Earl Robert became Justiciar as soon as Duke Henry became King Henry II in 1154."

"Okay, Cathy Chappell, you scored maximum points in our quiz. Your prize is an afternoon of passion with Chris Chappell."

"Earl Robert was now in charge of the administration of England... and King Henry was happy to have someone sort out all the in-fighting."

"I give up. Goodnight Cath. Even though it's only

half-three in the afternoon."

"Let's go back a bit. It's believed that Guy de Gaul was originally a sword for hire. He came up from the southwest of France and fought with Robert of Leicester when he was trying to regain lands in Normandy. Robert made Guy a knight and allowed him to build a castle in Leicestershire – although it had to be small, contain a hospital and a chapel, and oversee the safety of church lands."

"I said goodnight, Cath."

"In 1148, De Gaul Castle opened…"

"You're not related to Vic from the canal, are you?"

"Remember, Robert supported King Stephen against the Empress Matilda, meaning Guy de Gaul did likewise. Although, for Guy, we believe this might have been the first time he'd given a solemn oath as a knight…"

"I give up. Someone please lock me in the tower. No, actually, let's divert my passion into buying more collectibles."

12

Attention Citizens!

On Monday morning, Cathy and Kay met up in Castle Close and set off together for work. Cathy was getting a little concerned over Chris recently. He seemed to be acting differently. The thing with his international toy car dealership didn't make any sense. He'd never shown the slightest interest in collectibles and now he was talking about turning it into a career.

She wondered – was it possible for her husband to be having a mid-life crisis at thirty-three?

Reaching the High Street, she glanced up at the castle on the hill and felt the weight of history on her shoulders. Then her phone rang. It was Tina the journalist.

"Hi Tina. How are you?"

"I'm fine Cathy. How are you in the light of the castle closing? When will you be leaving for London? And could I get some inside info on the new plans for De Gaul?"

"It's not signed and sealed yet."

"I'm hearing it's all but done. Are you excited about the repairs and alterations?"

"Let me get back to you on that, Tina. Don't worry, I'll update you as soon as I can."

Cathy ended the call and puffed out her cheeks.

"Tina wants a story."

"She'll get it from Shane Tyler if she doesn't get it from you."

"It sounds like she already has. I just don't want to give up without trying to change his mind on closing down. If I go back to London, I'll never get back here. London does that to people."

"True. A friend of mine from school went there after university. Never came back."

"My plan is the best of both worlds. We get Tyler to carry out the repairs in stages so we can stay open for the public. Then we persuade him to let British Heritage run the tourism side of things for him. And then I get to stay on and unite the two regions when Pete Williams retires. It'll be really busy all the time, Kay. Plenty of work for all of us."

"We'll see," said Kay. "I'm not holding out much hope, to be honest. He only has to say the magic words – health and safety – and the old place will close in a flash."

"We need to persuade him a hundred percent then."

"How?"

"By getting the public to back us."

"The public? How?"

Cathy looked around, as if for inspiration. Then she saw it, stuck to a wall – a poster for an upcoming election rally at the community hall.

"We'll call a meeting. Tomorrow night at the community hall."

"Good idea, but Tuesdays at the hall is yoga night.

They won't shift for a meeting."

"Wednesday night then."

"Judo. You definitely won't shift them."

"Thursday night?"

"Bingo."

"Great, I'll pop in and book it."

"No, *bingo*. Thursday is senior citizens' bingo night."

"Right, forget the hall. We'll hold it at De Gaul. Tomorrow night at seven."

"How will we let people know?"

"We'll um…"

She looked at the poster again. Then an election van came rolling slowly by. Inside, an elderly man with a microphone was broadcasting through the bullhorn strapped to the roof. His message of economic renewal was lost on Cathy. His method of delivery, however, was not.

Around half-eleven, with a couple of volunteers in place to deal with visitors at the castle, Cathy and Kay slipped away to pick up the van.

"I'm sure this is a bad idea," said Kay.

"It's just a publicity drive, Kay. Nothing to it."

A short while later, they were setting off in the van, with Cathy looking more pleased with the situation than her friend.

"It was good of him to let us have it," said Cathy, stationed in the passenger seat holding the microphone.

"I think he's under the impression we're taking it for a wash," said Kay, turning out of the car park onto the High Street. "It's a good job I know his sister."

Cathy recalled the instructions for using the microphone. Press the button to speak, release to deactivate.

Easy-peasy.

"Calling all citizens of Castle Hill."

The sound of her amplified voice reverberated through the town, which she quite liked.

"Calling all citizens of Castle Hill. The aliens have landed."

Kay gasped. "What are you doing!"

Cathy smirked. "Sorry, couldn't resist."

"I thought you were serious about this?"

"Meeting tonight!" Cathy declared. "Please come to a meeting at De Gaul Castle tonight at seven p.m. We need your help to save De Gaul Castle from an insensitive developer. He's planning to knock it down and build apartments."

Kay screeched to a halt.

"You can't say that! It's not true."

"Kay, I only have one task while I'm sitting here, and that's to get people to the meeting. Now please drive on. I want to go around at least three times before we have to get the van back."

They set off again, but almost straightaway had to stop at the traffic lights.

"Citizens of Castle Hill. We are in a siege situation. A mediaeval war. Once again, it's 1135."

An old man passing by checked his watch.

"No, it's 11:45."

"Citizens, I urge you to attend a counter-offensive meeting at De Gaul Castle tomorrow evening at seven. We aren't just fighting for the castle, we're going into battle for the very soul of this community. Blood will be spilled… followed by tea and biscuits."

"That'll get 'em in," said Kay.

"Good. Let's just hope we don't get any miserable,

awkward timewasters turning up. Oh, hang on, I should have switched the mic off…"

13

A Little History

Chris was enjoying himself. Wearing wellies, he was with Dave, standing at the bottom of the empty lock between the main canal and the arm they hoped would one day be restored and lead to the lost pub and beyond.

"Anyone need a prosthetic leg?" he said, pulling one out of the silt and mud. "Unless this is just the start and we pull out an entire body."

"Chris? Are you self-employed?" asked Sam.

Chris looked up to the side of the lock where he feared an eight-year-old girl was about to ask some difficult questions.

"Yes, I am, Sam."

"My Uncle Kieran is self-employed but Mummy says he'll work himself into an early grave."

"Thankfully, this is a lock chamber, not a grave."

"Uncle Kieran should be more like you. You always make sure you take plenty of time off work."

"Yes… ahem… yes, absolutely. It's important to create what we self-employed people call a work-life balance."

That is, I'd like more work so I can balance my bank account.

"That's probably enough questions, Sam," Dave advised his daughter.

"Did I tell you about the Inland Waterways Association, Chris?" asked Vic, taking Sam's position on the lock side above them.

"Yes, you did, Vic," said Chris. *So no need to tell me again.*

"It was formed in 1946 to campaign for the canals."

"Yes, that's it. That's what you told me."

"Conservation, restoration, maintenance, access…"

"Look at the time," said Dave. "I'd better get us some lunch. A couple of cheese salad rolls, Chris?"

"Do you want me to come with you?"

"No, no, you can stay here with Vic."

"Great. *Thanks.*"

"Don't worry," said Dave, "you'll be able to continue your work-life balance on the Mary-Lou later."

Chris cheered up. It had been an unexpected invitation, but one he couldn't wait to take up. He'd handled a narrow boat in his early twenties, having driven one on a week-long Norfolk Broads holiday with his mates, but he still felt like an excited novice.

Ahh the bliss.

"In 1944, Tom Rolt published his book Narrow Boat," said Vic as Dave climbed out and strode off with Sam. "You *do* recall I mentioned it, Chris?"

"Yes, I distinctly remember you telling me."

"That's why you're in that lock, Chris. Because Tom and Angie Rolt went out on Cressy in 1939. Funny how the world works."

Chris stopped his shovelling for a moment.

"If you put it like that, then yes, it's a funny old world,

Vic. Now, I suppose I'd better get on…"

"Tom Rolt's description of the Victorian ways surviving into the 1930s on some of the canals struck a chord with a lot of people – one of them being Robert Aickman. You heard of him?"

Chris was shovelling now, only half-listening.

"No, can't say I have."

"He was a literary agent who came up with the idea of forming a campaign group. He met Tom Rolt aboard Cressy in 1946 at a place called Tardebigge on the Worcester and Birmingham Canal."

"Interesting…"

"Next thing you know, they had the inaugural meeting of The Inland Waterways Association at Aickman's flat in Gower Street, London."

"Right…"

"The first action took place in 1947, Chris. The Rolts aboard Cressy took on the Great Western Railway."

Chris paused. "The railway? I thought you were talking about canals, Vic."

"The railway company owned the Stratford-upon-Avon Canal – and they got rid of the Lifford drawbridge at Kings Norton Junction."

"Right."

"Do you know what they did next?"

"No idea, Vic."

Chris decided to let Vic talk himself out. In a few minutes, peace would be restored and he'd be able to get back to clearing sludge.

"They put in a temporary fixed bridge, Chris – but it was too low across the water to allow boats under. Well, that's why they had a drawbridge in the first place – so it could be raised to let boats through."

"Yes, I see," said Chris, wondering if it would be

possible to dig a tunnel to escape Vic's lecture.

"Anyway, the Rolts got support and had a question raised in Parliament by Lord Methuen. It took a while, but that daft new bridge was removed and the magnificent Cressy was eventually able to pass along the canal unhindered."

"Good ol' Cressy."

"You see, it was the start of something. A message had been issued to the authorities. Keep your dead hand of bureaucracy off our canals!"

"Were you there at that time, Vic?"

"Not at that time, no. But we'll get to that."

Oh crap.

Chris got back to his work while Vic's memories fought a war against the canal owners. It was while he was describing, in detail, the narrow boat Ailsa Craig's cruise of the northern canals during the summer of 1948, that another member of the Tow-Path Taskforce came by.

"Hello Caroline," said Chris.

"Hi."

"I was just telling Chris about the Ailsa Craig," said Vic. "He's keen to learn more. Unless you want to perform your thing right away."

"No, I'll wait till you're finished."

Chris was puzzled.

"What thing?" he asked.

Caroline smiled. "It's a blessing."

"A blessing?" Chris was none the wiser.

"Caroline's a witch," said Vic. "Anyway, I was telling you about the Ailsa Craig. Do you know—"

"Whoa, hang on a sec. A witch?"

"Yes, anyway, that was the last crossing of the Huddersfield Narrow Canal for over fifty years. It wasn't until it was restored by heroes in 2001 that you got another boat through it."

Chris wondered if he'd fallen asleep and now had a role in Alice in Wonderland. Either that, or this was about to turn into The Wicker Man.

"Can we get back to the witch thing?" he asked to be sure.

"Caroline's a white witch," said Vic. "One of the best."

Chris looked to Caroline for reassurance, but she just laughed.

"What's it involve?" he asked. "Boiling frogs and making broomsticks?"

"That's just at weekends," said Caroline. "During the week, I work for the police."

"Oh... you mean you help them solve crimes?"

"No, I work in the admin office. This is my lunch break."

"Ah right... and do you ever wear the outfit?"

"No, it's only the police officers who wear a uniform. Admin staff have to be smart-casual."

"No, I meant..."

"I know what you meant. Just so you know, long flowing robes are optional."

"A white witch. How unusual."

"I'm quite normal. I've even got a mortgage. And we don't actually call ourselves witches."

"Right, so definitely no broomsticks then?"

"No."

"No nipping off for a quick game of quidditch?"

"I'd never make the team."

Chris climbed out of the lock.

"You might as well do your thing then, Caroline. I need a break."

Caroline looked down into the lock and then up to the

sky.

"Bless the past, bless the present, and bless the future. Let this place of passage, of journeying, be open once again, and be ever blessed with positive energy…"

Chris wandered away from the lock to the edge of the main canal, where a narrow boat was passing. The sign on the side caught his eye. 'For Sale'.

He wanted it. Although, he guessed a nice vessel like that would cost a fortune. But he definitely wanted a boat. He would call it 'Living The Dream' and he and Cathy would have a touch of the simple life, with lots of slow cruising, and the occasional stop at a canal-side pub. It would give them some much-needed respite from their work. Well, it would give Cathy respite. Chris wasn't quite so much in need of that.

His friend Ian popped into his head. Ian's wife Debbie was a busy high school head teacher and spent all her time absorbed by her career, while Ian put less and less effort into his one man painting & decorating business on account of Debbie's very good income. When Ian insisted they use most of their joint savings to buy a sixty grand sports car, she divorced him.

Chris let the narrow boat drift out of view.

Two hours later, having finished his shift with Dave, Chris made his way home. For some reason, Vic set off alongside him talking about the Inland Waterways Association.

By the church, Chris paused.

"Don't you have any other interests, Vic? Aside from the history of the canals, I mean?"

"Of course I do. Have I ever told you about the Great Storm of 1703?"

Please don't.

"It was a terror, Chris."

"Yes, I've heard of it."

"Not the half of it, I'd wager. Trees, chimney stacks – you name it, they all came down that day. In London, the lead roofing was blown off Westminster Abbey. In Cambridge, the pinnacles were blown from the top of King's College Chapel. Ships? They were smashed to pieces with a terrible loss of life. The Church of England said it was God's punishment meted out to a sinful nation. You know Daniel Defoe, the man who wrote Robinson Crusoe?"

"Er…?"

"He said it was God's retribution for underperformance against the Catholics in the War of the Spanish Succession."

"Right, well…"

"Do you know the worst of it was right here in the Midlands?"

"No, I didn't, but…"

"Hurricane winds, severe flooding… the old wooden town hall was smashed to pieces. What survived was washed away by the flood."

Chris spotted two familiar figures in the small graveyard looking at the stones.

"Oh look, Vic – it's Jasmine and Grace." He called out. "Hello, you two! I'd have thought you'd have covered every inch of this place by now."

"Yes, like my dad before me," Grace called back. "He never found anything either."

"No luck with the parish council records then?"

Chris knew that Jasmine's dad had spent many years on that grand body, meaning she could get access.

"The records aren't old enough, Chris. We think the

earlier ones were most likely lost in the flood of 1703."

"Funny you should say that," said Vic.

Oh gawd…

"Why don't we join them, Vic," said Chris, already setting off to do just that.

"I won't," said Vic. "I've got a couple of errands to run."

In the graveyard, minus Vic, Chris saw that Jasmine and Grace were studying a particular gravestone.

"My great, great, great, great, great grandad," said Grace. "And don't ask me to say that again – my teeth might fly out."

"Josiah Lincoln," Chris intoned on reading the name on the stone. "1742 to 1799." He noticed a weathered flower symbol carved into the stone.

"That's as far back as we can go," said Jasmine. "We've tried the nearby parishes too. No luck."

"How's Cathy?" Grace asked.

Chris refocused. "Oh, she's fine."

"We'll be sorry to lose you," said Jasmine.

"Thanks, but it's not final yet. Cathy won't give up without a fight."

"I think we worked that out," said Jasmine.

"And I'll be fighting alongside her," he added.

"We worked that out, too," said Grace.

14

Can I Count On Your Support?

Not far off sunset, the sky above was mostly clear — although the wind had picked up from the southwest, which usually meant clouds were on the way. From the top of the keep at De Gaul Castle, Chris stood on the proclamation spot where, in centuries past, news of a local tax hike would be issued to the local populace. That's why the wall was higher here — to protect the proclaimer from getting an arrow up the throat.

Below him, two townsfolk were coming up the hill. How many would that make it in total? Seven? Eight?

He checked his watch. It was already ten-to-seven.

Chris stepped back inside the building. The upper floors, he felt, were very atmospheric. If you were there alone long enough, the mind could easily play tricks.

What was that noise?

He hurried down the stairs to the grand hall, where Cathy was hanging around looking pensive. Kay was there too, along with a few locals and someone from the local business community. A moment later, the two people Chris had seen duly arrived, meaning Cathy had almost the whole town not there for the meeting.

She came over.

"I need your one hundred percent support on this."

"You don't have to go through with it, Cath."

"That's not one hundred percent."

He lured her away to a corner for privacy.

"What's so bad about going back to London? We don't have to constantly see your baby-obsessed friends, or even your sister. And we don't have to bother with IVF either. We can just move on with our lives."

"Chris, if we go back to London, we *do* have to go through it again. Even though I've lost faith in it."

Chris sighed and tried to put an arm around her, but she pulled away. It made him feel useless.

"I have to stay and fight," said Cathy. "For all we know, I could be the great, great times a hundred granddaughter of Guy de Gaul."

"Neither of us believes that, Cath. Your grandad's a drink-addled fibber."

"It was passed down to him through the family – and do not say my entire line were drunks and liars."

"I'm just saying..."

"Somebody has to be related to the people who built this place. And don't forget, I feel it in my bones every time I enter that courtyard."

"You sound like Caroline, the White Witch of the West... West Leicestershire Police Force, that is."

"What?"

"Another time."

"Look, I need to stop Tyler from shutting this place down. If I don't succeed, we'll go back to London. Okay?"

"Okay, I suppose... I'm also okay with staying here and you finding another job. Just so you know."

"Thanks, but you know full well I'm not stepping outside of history. It's my career and my passion. We can beat this guy, Chris. Hopefully, he'll discover that when he hears what tonight's meeting thinks of his plans."

Chris looked over her shoulder towards the entrance.

"I reckon he'll hear about it pretty soon, Cath. He's just walked in with that local journalist friend of yours."

Before long, the meeting got under way with Cathy welcoming everyone to this most important public debate. Kay nodded alongside her. Chris would have too, but Kay suggested he give his support from the audience in case the public felt outnumbered by the panel.

Still, Cathy knew he was there, supporting her. He knew she probably wouldn't get her dream job back, but he loved her and would back her to the hilt, even though she had clearly lost her marbles.

"The question before us," Cathy announced, "is do we want this precious resource taken away from this community for a whole year? I say we don't. I say we can get the developer..." she glanced at Shane Tyler who was sitting at the back, looking at his phone, "...to agree to a staged restoration, whereby the work is carried out over a longer period, say two years, thus allowing public access to most of the castle all of the time."

A hand went up in the audience, just in front of Chris. It was an elderly man in a raincoat and trilby hat who smelled of cigarettes.

"Yes, please do speak, sir," said Cathy.

"Have you seen that crack over the arch at the front?"

"Yes, we're aware of the crack. I understand some

underpinning of one side will stop it worsening. Then we can repair it and make it look as good as new."

"Who exactly is we?" the man asked. "British Heritage has had it for years and done absolutely nothing."

Chris felt like telling him not to be so rude.

"We've had limited funds, of course," said Cathy, "but every penny goes into maintenance and restoration."

Another hand went up.

"Yes madam?"

"You won't raise the kind of money this place needs with a fete and a few raffle tickets."

"We would hope to call on Mr Tyler's funds for the bulk of the work."

Another hand.

"I'm Mrs Harrington, a member of the parish council."

Chris had run into Mrs Harrington a couple of times in the local shops. She gave the impression of having arrived by time machine from 1912.

"Yes, Mrs Harrington – your point?"

"As long as it's not turned into Disneyland, I don't see an issue with a new owner making bold decisions. If he's received expert architectural and structural engineering opinion that De Gaul must close for a year, I fail to see how your qualification as a historian puts you in a position to argue against that advice."

"Yes, well, we have yet to engage our own structural engineer. This meeting is purely to gauge the mood of the people."

Chris felt they were gauging that quite accurately.

"Marta Verhoff from the bakery in the High Street," said voice behind Chris. "Anything that boosts visitor numbers in the long term is in the best interests of everyone in Castle Hill. If that's best achieved with a short-term closure, I'd have no objections."

"With the site manager's permission," said an Australian voice from somewhere at the back, "I'd like to address my comments to the people from the town who came out tonight. I'm Shane Tyler, the new owner of De Gaul Castle. Please don't crane your necks, I'll come to the front."

Cathy looked set to protest, but Shane Tyler was already on the move. To add insult to injury, he stood directly in front of her, largely blocking her out from the tiny audience.

Chris didn't like that at all.

"The main thing is money," said Tyler.

"The main thing is history," said Cathy moving to one side of her foe.

"The main thing is having the money to save the history," said Tyler.

"Obviously money is important but without an understanding of history, we could end up making poor choices on how to spend the money."

"My ancestors built this castle," said Tyler. "My duty is to the heritage they have passed down to me."

"The evidence is yet to be seen on that – and I'm sure audience members don't wish to see us arguing."

"It beats what's on TV," said the man in the trilby.

Chris felt like taking the stupid hat and treading on it.

"I've never been afraid to fight for what's right," said Shane Tyler. "Long before I made money, I knew I would restore this castle and my family's name along with it."

"The people deserve a chance to visit the castle anytime they want between the first of March and the end of October. For children, it's their right, but, as ever, it's children's rights that are the first to go. So we're led *once more unto the breaching* of those rights."

"This will become a world class visitor experience."

"We must fight this arrogance in this meeting. We must fight it in the town…"

"I'll give a free one-year pass to every local citizen."

"Rising from your beds, months from now, would you be willing to trade access this year for a pass for next year? Or would you prefer to tell Mr Tyler he may take our castle, but he'll never take our freedom to enter it."

Chris sighed. Shakespeare, Churchill, Braveheart… what next?

"Nam et ipsa scientia potestas est," said Cathy. "Knowledge is power."

"Vincit qui patitur," said Tyler. "Patience wins. It's my family motto."

"Show me your hands!" said Cathy. "All those with me to keep this place open the whole time – raise them now."

Chris and Kay raised theirs.

Tyler took up the challenge. "All those who want to see a world class visitor experience, even if it means shutting down for a year?"

All other hands went up.

"We close in two weeks," said Shane Tyler. "This castle will be the pride and joy of the region. And you're all invited to the grand reopening champagne reception."

Tyler left the platform and the building, and the meeting duly broke up.

Chris couldn't face Cathy straightaway, so he stepped outside for some air – where Kay had waylaid Tyler.

Chris stayed back in the shadows.

"Maybe there's a compromise?" she asked.

"Are you a historian, Kay?"

"I know a little."

"You know the Earl of Leicester supported Stephen. You believe Guy de Gaul supported the Earl. Have you heard of Paul Courtenay?"

"Yes, he was a minor figure who supported Matilda."

"I found a reference – a bit vague – but showing the Courtenays had a raven emblem and held an estate in this region."

"A lot of the history is vague, especially the further you get from the main players."

"When the Earl switched his support from Stephen to Matilda's son, Henry, where do you think that left the de Gauls?"

"With a choice of sticking with Stephen or switching to the man who would soon become Henry II."

"And what if the Courtenays and de Gauls were on different sides and fought each other?"

"There are no records I know of."

"Yes, annoying, isn't it, but it might be the Courtenays built this castle, not the de Gauls. That's significant."

"Is it? It sounds more like speculation."

"I have a letter written by my ancestor Jeremiah Dupris and he has a raven emblem printed on the letter heading."

"So you might be related to a line that didn't build the castle?"

"What if the de Gauls were the aggressors? It could be the castle is wrongly named. Remember, what little we know suggests the de Gauls were mercenaries."

"Yes, but Guy de Gaul became a knight."

"Hmm… we'll see."

"You can't rename the castle, Mr Tyler."

"Kay, you have an impressive grasp of history. How come you're not the site manager?"

"You're forgetting – Henry Hume was the site

manager for thirty-two years. Then Cathy came up here with a plan to merge two regions."

"Yes, but British Heritage are handing over to me."

"True."

"Listen, I'm staying at the Red Lion Hotel. Why not come along? We could have a drink and a bite to eat… and discuss your future."

Chris slipped away. Tyler was a predator. He would love and leave women on a weekly basis.

Poor Kay.

He rejoined Cathy – and he felt roused. A sleeping giant was awakening. Finally, he knew what kind of partner he needed to be – one who stepped in and started throwing his weight around.

"It's my turn for a crack at him, Cath. I'll sort him out."

"How?"

"I'll use a bit of psychology."

"Don't be ridiculous."

"I'm serious."

"No, I'll get him. I just need to take it to the next level. Me and Kay versus Tyler. He doesn't stand a chance."

On the hill, overlooking the river, Hugh de Gaul sensed a change. Treachery, no doubt. There was certainly something in the air. The easy way. For some, it always held the greater appeal. He would have to be vigilant if he had any hope of holding on.

15

How To Beat Shane Tyler

Chris pondered many things over his cereal the following morning – mainly letting Cathy get on with attacking Tyler from the front while he worked out a more subtle way to bring his wife's nemesis to order. No more being a passenger in their marriage. He would be taking a turn at the wheel and plotting a smarter route.

He felt bad about not letting on that Kay might be on the verge of becoming a double agent, though – but he couldn't start making accusations about a woman he liked and admired on the basis of a sneaky bit of eavesdropping.

"Right, so you accept I'm the right man for the job," he said, "and that I'll come up with the single best way to get Tyler to compromise. Agreed?"

The cat looked at him then left the kitchen.

"Thanks for the vote."

The sound of Cathy coming downstairs had him ready to repeat his statement of intent.

"Why's your fishing gear by the front door?"

"Oh come on, we'll be gone before long. I'm just getting a summer's worth in while we're here."

"I thought you were working for a new client?"

"I am. I'm just waiting for him to get back to me. Anyway, let's talk about Tyler. It's my turn to have a crack at him."

"People don't take turns when it's life or death, Chris. Besides, I've got Kay on my side."

Chris resisted the urge to be a lowlife sneak.

"I've already started, Cath, so at least listen. According to my research on Wikipedia, Shane Tyler's a keen sailor. In fact, he was in the Americas Cup. That's ocean yacht racing."

"I know what the Americas Cup is."

"Anyway, with that in mind, I'm wondering if I might get him interested in the canal."

Cathy stared at him in much the way you might stare at a poodle dressed as Elvis Presley.

"You're going to fish out dead dogs together?"

"Now hold on, that's a good canal. Very clean thanks to us volunteers. All I'm saying is we need to win him over with engagement not fighting."

"How?"

"Okay, so Tyler's into boats…"

"Yes, ocean-racing yachts that cost squillions."

"…so, I was thinking I'll get him into narrow boats. Great, eh?"

"No, it's rubbish."

"How can you say that?"

"Chris, just leave this to me."

"Okay, but this won't involve raising another army of townsfolk against him, will it?"

"From what I know, we just have to prove he's not

linked to the castle – then he'll go away."

"But if he's not linked, he might pull out altogether. Then the castle would lose big money. Nobody wants that, Cath. Including you."

"One thing at a time. I'll make sure the castle doesn't lose its money."

"How?"

"You'll just have to wait and see. First we need to prove Tyler's no Norman knight."

"I give up."

"No, never give up, Chris. Look, I've bookmarked a couple of my own Norman link prospects on the laptop. I haven't had a chance to look at them properly. You can help."

"Yes, Your Ladyship."

Chris made some coffee while Cathy fired up her machine. A few minutes later they were sitting down to one of Cathy's Victorian ancestors.

"Who's this?" said Chris, peering at the screen. "Oliver Craig…?"

"Yes, according to the 1871 census, he was living in Nottingham, which isn't a million miles from Castle Hill. He was a cousin of the Barretts, I think. Have a look at the entry."

"That's weird," said Chris, peering at the handwritten entry. "Cousin Oliver seems to have lived with loads of other men at the same address."

"Really?"

"Well, it's dittos all the way down. Let's try going back a page… more dittos… and more… ah, there's the address. Nottingham Prison."

"Are you sure you haven't skipped a page?"

"It's all there in photocopied black and white."

"Maybe he was the prison chief?"

"No, if you look at the first one at the top of the page, it says 'inmate'. That doesn't sound like an official title – and that ditto symbol goes down the page against all of them, including, Oliver Craig. He was in jail, Cath."

"Maybe he was wrongly accused. Or perhaps he was a political prisoner? A prisoner of conscience?"

"Whatever you say."

"Will you still love me if it turns out I'm from a criminal family."

"Yes, but you might lose all your land and titles."

Chris got up and headed to the kitchen.

Cathy followed him to the toaster.

"Actually, now I think of it," she said, "do you remember that time Mum got drunk?"

"You'll need to narrow that down a bit," said Chris cutting some bread off yesterday's loaf.

"She said the Craigs were a useless bunch."

"Did she?"

"I was our designated driver, so I was stone cold sober and had to listen to the whole thing. She said when she was six Uncle Stan Craig stole her piggy-bank."

"To help fund a children's charity...?" said Chris without any obvious belief as he popped the cut bread into the toaster.

"Look," said Cathy. "Tyler's the one we need to nail with rubbish ancestors, okay?"

"Cath, we've just established you're related to Ollie the Outlaw. Why don't you let me have a crack at Tyler? I'm sure I could get him to calm down and see there might be a compromise to be had."

"No, we need to keep our focus on the Two-fold Tyler Challenge. If his family—"

"Where the hell did that come from? The Two-fold Tyler Challenge? You make it sound like a game show."

"We have to prove he's not linked to the people who built the castle, but we also have to make him love the history to the point he's still keen to spend big money on it. Then we have to make him see it's only right to keep it open during the renovation work."

Chris was retrieving the butter from the fridge.

"Surely that's a Three-fold Tyler Challenge?"

"Stop being silly."

"Me?"

Sometimes Chris wished the castle had never been built.

"Shame they didn't have canal boats in the 12th Century," he said. "Then they might have been a little more civilized."

Twenty minutes later, they were heading up to the High Street – Cathy bound for work and Chris with his fishing gear making his intentions for the morning fairly clear.

"Of course there is another solution," he said. "We could sell up and live on a narrow boat."

"Why would we do that?"

"Adventure?"

"No."

"Think of it. We'd have total freedom. We could call our boat Living the Dream."

"That's not total freedom, Chris. It's also a daft name."

"It *is* total freedom, Cath. We wouldn't need a thing."

"Apart from a canal license and money for mooring fees. And don't you need insurance? You'd probably need a safety certificate, too. And fuel for the engine and the cooker. Then there's maintenance, signing on with a doctor, beer money…"

"Yeah, okay, so not *total* freedom then."

"It was boats that caused all the chaos in the first place," said Cathy. "I've told you about the White Ship, haven't I?"

"Er...?" He did recall some reference to a white ship.

"The ship that sank, drowning Henry the First's sole heir? Cousins Stephen and Matilda at each other's throats over who would take the crown?"

"Yes, now you've said it, it does ring a bell."

Cathy huffed. "I listen to all your fishing talk. You never pay a minute's attention to my passion."

"No, well... yes... the White Ship. Fascinating stuff."

"It caused a civil war, Chris. One boat."

"I get the same from Vic on the canal with his talks on Cressy. If it weren't for that boat, we wouldn't have any canals today. Did you know that?"

"I'm talking about history, Chris."

"So is Vic."

"Yes... yes, he is. Except you usually tell me how Vic keeps going on and on about it. Or is that how you see me too? Do I keep going on and on about it?"

"No, of course not. It's your job."

"And with Vic?"

"Well, it seems to be his entire life."

"Passion is good, Chris."

"I do listen, Cath. I know the White Ship set sail in... 1168?"

"1120."

"And one of the Henrys was king?"

"Henry I."

"And his only heir died at sea?"

"His only legitimate son, William Adelin."

"And this was... Dover?"

"Barfleur, France. It set sail after a drunken pub

party."

"And Stephen and Matilda spent years at each other's throats?"

"Not straight away. While Henry I was alive, everyone agreed Matilda should take over when he died."

"Right, then Henry died and everyone changed their mind?"

"Stephen did. He was on the first boat to England pulling the crown onto his head."

"Well, there you go, Cath. I do know my history."

"It doesn't help much with proving Tyler isn't linked to the castle."

"Well, Jasmine's the fourth genealogist he's had on this, so he's not getting very far on his side of the argument."

"And doesn't that suggest it might not be him linked to the castle, but someone else. Someone like me, perhaps?"

"I was thinking more along the lines of... Grace?"

"Yes, well, it could be Grace. I wouldn't mind that at all. She wouldn't close the castle down."

"No, she wouldn't. Although carrying out a multi-million pound restoration is never easy on a state pension."

Cathy pondered it. "Grace has taken her family tree a lot farther back than anyone else."

"I know. Have you seen the gravestones in the churchyard? Hey! Why don't you have a look up there? You might find one of yours."

"What, in the graveyard?"

"Yes."

"I hate those places. They give me the creeps."

"You could go now... a quick fifteen-minute detour before work. You could text Kay and say you'll be late?"

"I suppose. You'll have to come with me, though. I'm not going alone."

"Why not?"

"It's a graveyard."

"Cath, it's nine in the morning, not midnight."

A few minutes later, Cathy and Chris were peering at gravestones in the hope of spotting a Barrett or a Craig. It was hard work though. Many of the stones were weather worn.

Ultimately, while they were unsuccessful, Chris came across two of Grace's family. One with a flower motif, one without. That puzzled him.

"Why don't we try inside?" he suggested. "See what the vicar knows."

They didn't even get to the front door of the church, when the Reverend Collins came out, seemingly on his way somewhere.

"Vicar?" said Chris. "I don't suppose you know if you're storing any Barretts or Craigs here, do you?"

The vicar looked preoccupied. "Off the top of my head, I can't say one way or the other. If you pop back this afternoon, I could have a look at our records."

"Perfect," said Chris. "There you go, Cath. All arranged."

The vicar hurried off and Cathy thrust her hands into her jacket pockets.

"I'm going to work," she said. "Maybe I'll drag Kay and Jasmine out for lunch. I've got a bit of an idea forming."

"An idea? Sounds dangerous."

She kissed Chris. "I do love you, you know."

"I love you too, you weirdo."

"Don't fall in the water."

"Don't get arrested."

Chris watched her go and wondered what nuttiness was forming in her head. Then he made his way to the canal. He supposed he should have told her he'd spotted a phone number on the business card Tyler gave her. And who knew Tyler would reply so promptly to a text and agree to meet up on the tow-path ten minutes from now?

16

A Fresh Approach

Chris arrived at the canal, took in a deep lungful of fresh air, saluted a passing blackbird, and set up his rod and line. It was important for Shane Tyler to find him looking incredibly relaxed.

He felt good about taking a more hands-on approach. For someone who didn't particularly believe in fate, he'd certainly lived a life where that's exactly what he'd left his destination to. Perched on his fold-up seat, he looked forward to trying a different approach to tame Cathy's nemesis.

He breathed in another lungful of fresh air. Maybe it wasn't just his attitude to the Shane Tyler problem that had shifted. Wasn't his entanglement with Castle Hill strengthening a little too? Thanks mainly to the canal and the small community of people who cared for it? He knew he'd stay on for Cathy's sake, but for his own?

He'd always lived on the northern fringe of London, but never actively engaged with Oxford Circus,

Buckingham Palace or Theatre-land. Whenever he took time off work, he'd jump in the car and drive north, away from London, towards the Hertfordshire countryside where the rivers and canals offered endless peaceful fishing.

He checked his watch. It wasn't far off Tyler time.

He looked along the tow-path to the slope that came down from the road by the old bridge.

Oh great…

"Morning Chris."

"Morning Vic."

"Caught anything?"

"Not yet, but we live in hope."

Vic came to a halt beside him. Chris's eyes remained fixed on his inert float.

"A wonderful public resource, these canals," said Vic.

Here we go…

"I told you about the Inland Waterways Association, didn't I?"

"Yes, Vic, you did." *At great length.*

"Yes, good people. I mean the roads were vital, but why lose the waterways?"

"Indeed."

"Mind you, the canals were in a bad way back then. The law stated boats could use them, but in practice most of the waterways weren't navigable. That was the ammunition the authorities tried to use against keeping the canals open. They wanted to close them all and fill them with concrete. You'd have trouble fishing in concrete, Chris."

"Yes indeed."

"You've got the Inland Waterways Association to thank for that."

"Yes, I fully appreciate the work the IWA did back in

the old days. As you say, they were good people."

"Did I mention how Tom Rolt and Robert Aickman toured the canals and found so many of the locks inoperative? And how they decided it was time for direct action?"

"No, but... ah, here comes Mr Tyler. You missed a good meeting last night, Vic. Mr Tyler made it known that the castle would be closing down for a whole year. What do you think of that?"

"I haven't been up there in forty years, Chris, so it doesn't really affect me."

"Forty years? But you only live two hundred yards from it."

"Never been interested in history. Boring, if you ask me."

"Mr Tyler, hello," Chris called out.

The approaching Shane Tyler was less than twenty yards away.

"I'll be on my way," said Vic. "You have a good day, Chris."

"And you, Vic."

He watched Vic head off down the tow-path, countryside bound. Then he turned the other way.

Tyler was upon him.

"Hello Chris. Thanks for getting in touch. I'm as keen as you are to make Cathy see sense. What's our first move?"

Right...

"I think our first move is to show her how much you care for the community."

"Oh? Why would we do that? Apart from it being good PR for me, I mean?"

"If Cathy saw you doing good things for the community, she would concede the moral high ground to you. Basically, she'd pack up and leave Castle Hill."

"Is that what you want?"

"Yes, I can't wait to get back to London. Oxford Circus? Buckingham Palace? Theatre-land? I miss it all, Shane. In fact, I'm setting up a collectibles business there. Old toy cars and so on. It's my passion."

"Well, I can understand that. I admire anyone who has a passion for what they do. So what's the plan?"

"I'd suggest making some small gesture. I mean... oh, I don't know... let's take where we're standing. Just up the canal there, there's an arm of water that used to run down to serve the old factories. Now that stretch could be reopened and developed, but first it would need new lock gates and a lot of clearing."

Tyler looked up and down the waterway.

"How fast are those narrow boats?" he asked.

"My friend Dave has a good one. The Mary-Lou. She's got a bit of pace. You try walking the tow-path alongside her when she's on the move and... well, you'd obviously keep up, but if you were to stop and talk to someone for twenty minutes, that boat would be out of sight. Whoosh. Gone."

Tyler laughed, but not for long.

"You know the reason I'm in Castle Hill, Chris. Tell me about Cathy. How did she get tied up with British Heritage?"

"She studied History at A-level and was offered a place at Exeter University to do a degree."

"Smart move."

"No, she went to Cornwall for a week, ended up staying the summer and fell in with a crowd who were going travelling come September. You know, Thailand to Tibet, kind of thing. Exeter could wait a year. Except her travelling only lasted until November and she never got beyond Thailand. By then she'd run out of money, so it was a return to London and a spot of job-hunting. But what about you, Shane. You're a boat man, aren't you? I saw a thing about the Americas Cup."

"You're not wrong, mate. I do love boats."

Tyler went on to talk about ocean-going yachts that sounded incredibly expensive. At the first opportunity, Chris switched the conversation away from multi-millionaires racing each other.

"So when did you first learn about your connection to De Gaul?"

"That's a while back, Chris. I must have been seven or eight. My parents brought me to England and we came up to look at the castle. It was my dad who said his ancestors owned the place."

"Did he say when?"

"He said our lot went all the way back to the beginning."

"Hmm, same as Cathy's grandad. So what would happen if your research proved you weren't connected to its early days?"

"I can't entertain that idea, Chris. No, it's our castle and it needs some TLC."

"And there's no way to persuade you to keep it open while the repairs take place?"

"No, I'm closing everything down. For the next year, the old place will be for ghosts and builders only."

Chris nodded. It was time for a spot of clever psychology. Luckily, he'd read just the thing in a magazine while waiting to have his hair cut.

"What's your view on otters, Shane?"

"Otters?"

The idea was to ask an obscure question and see how the other person dealt with it.

"Why do you ask?"

That wasn't what Chris wanted to hear. A big success like Shane Tyler was meant to be dismissive, leaving himself open to Chris explaining the health of the otter population as an important topic. Then Tyler would say sorry and be on the back foot.

"You an otter man, Chris?" Tyler started laughing. "Ottoman, get it? It's a kind of storage seat."

"Forget all that for minute, Shane – why don't you let me get a few boat people together. You could listen to their thoughts on the local canals. You don't need to spend money on old locks, but it wouldn't hurt you to engage with the community."

"Well…"

"Their goodwill towards you would radiate far and wide, Shane."

"Hmm…"

"Don't say no before you've seen the boats gathered. I'm sure you'll be impressed."

"Okay, you've got my number. I'm only in town for a few more days though – then it's off to America for a month or two."

"Leave it with me."

Watching Shane Tyler head off along the tow-path back to civilization, Chris wondered what kind of 'boat thing' would impress him. Clearly, he needed to think big.

Then he wondered why he'd bragged to Tyler about setting up a collectibles business when it wasn't true.

Or maybe it was true and he hadn't yet grasped how smart the idea was. Of course, he could easily imagine Cathy going all Freudian and saying it represented a need to have kids. But he would insist it was his new passion.

But it wouldn't be true. He didn't have a genuine passion for it. Or for anything else. Was it possible to live a whole lifetime devoid of passion? Just drifting by slowly, like an old narrow boat?

That afternoon, Cathy left the church with a total failure to find her ancestors. Putting the disappointment swiftly behind her, she went to meet Kay in the play park. As hoped, Kay had brought the homemade placards and gathered together three mothers and their small children.

"Tina should be here soon," she said.

As if on cue, local reporter Tina and a photographer pulled up across the road and joined them.

While Cathy handed out the placards, she explained how local kids were about to be deprived of a vital educational facility for a whole year. The new owner's obsession with closing the castle down would mean all school visits being called off.

Tina recorded the interview and they got photos of the parents with children holding protest placards – and with De Gaul Castle looking distant but relevant in the background. The only surprise for Cathy was being asked to swell the ranks of the protesters for a photo and having a baby thrust into her arms by a mother of twins.

17

It's Like This…

With the castle closed for a few days of assessment, Cathy was working from home on the Tuesday morning. She was seated facing Chris at the kitchen table with their laptops back to back.

"He's got a cheek," she muttered. "It's the start of the Easter holidays… thousands of schoolkids at a loose end… thousands of parents looking for things to do… and we're closed for business."

"It'll reopen Thursday or Friday," said Chris.

"Yeah, for a week or two, then bam."

"Plenty of time to get used to the idea of going back to London. Unless you've re-thought the idea of getting another job up here?"

"Damn!"

"Now what?"

"It's the castle's anniversary."

"Today?"

"No, not today. Well, it might be today. Who knows?

No, I mean it was built in 1148, so well worth a big celebration, right?"

"It doesn't sound like a major milestone, Cath. I'd imagine the one thousandth anniversary would get a bit of coverage on the news, but eight hundred and whatever…"

"I've already got the Three Counties Re-enactment Society on standby."

"Not those nuts who re-hash Norman sieges?"

"They have authentic outfits and everything."

"Well, they'll have to miss a year."

"Chris, these people have been doing it for centuries. Well, since 2003."

Chris stood up.

"I'm going to grab a shower."

Cathy grumbled and took her laptop into the lounge. On the sofa, she logged into her regular genealogy site. Within seconds, half the keyboard was obscured by a laptop cat.

"What's up, TT? Aren't there any pigeons to be stared at through the window?"

Despite the obstacle, Cathy found the page she wanted – the Barrett line on her mother's side who had lived in the Midlands in Victorian times.

According to the 1861 census, nineteen-year-old sawmill worker Frederick Barrett was residing in Castle Hill. Of course, Cathy had come across him before, but had yet to find any trace of him prior to this date. Why wasn't he in the 1851 census? That was the question.

The doorbell rang.

It was Kay.

"Grace says it feels like a coffee and pastries morning? She's just getting ready so we've got about half an hour. Fancy it?"

"Come in, Kay. I just need five minutes then we'll go and drag her out."

Cathy showed Kay into the lounge, where Kay met a furry object now sprawled along the sofa by the abandoned laptop.

"Hello TT – doing important relaxation research again?" Kay leaned down to scratch Truly-Trudy behind the ears. "Or are you just a lazy fur-ball?"

Truly-Trudy's eyes closed.

"Homework?" said Kay, eyeing the laptop.

"Waste of time, more like," said Cathy. "It's my family in 1861. Specifically, Frederick the sawmill guy. He seems to have beamed down from the Starship Enterprise though, because there's no earlier record of him."

Kay squinted at the online photocopy of the handwritten original entry.

"This scrawl is worse than mine... is that your boy? Frederick Barnett?"

"No, Barrett."

Cathy's brain was already working on what to wear when it experienced a gear-crunching, skid-to-a-halt.

"Barnett..." she uttered.

"I though you said Barrett."

"Yes, but... well, we look at copies of the original documents, but when it comes to searching, we go into an online database someone has transcribed from the original handwritten scrawl."

"Oh, and you think...?"

"With a bit of luck, Kay, you might have got me one step closer to my castle ancestors. I'll check it out later."

Twenty minutes later, Cathy, Kay and Grace were snugly installed in *La Cucina*, a small Italian café-restaurant on the High Street. While getting acquainted with their coffees and pastries, Cathy peered out of the window where, between the White Horse pub and the Foxglove Tea Rooms, De Gaul Castle peered back at her from the hill.

"I don't want to go back to London," she sighed.

"We know," said Grace.

"It's not just the castle keeping me here. Castle Hill has given me the distance I needed from other things."

But Cathy didn't want to mention the failed business of becoming a mother. She didn't want to say how she felt like a musician prevented from playing, or an artist denied a brush and paint. She was the dreamer without hope. Someone's whose vivid cinematic thought-movie of her and Chris and their children had begun the process of fading.

She couldn't hold it in any longer.

And yet she had to. She could imagine the conversation, telling them how she feared London would mean another IVF failure. Grace would sympathize. Kay might apologize for showing all those photos and videos of her baby niece. But when people learn you're going through IVF it inspires them to tell you to relax and let it happen. Or to think positive and let it happen. Or to try hypnotherapy, reflexology, Vitamin C, Vitamin D, green tea, and sugar-free. Then a week later they ask 'any news?'

Yes, she had to hold in how she would be unconscious on a table, her feet in stirrups, with a crowd of medical staff staring at her. She couldn't say how Chris wouldn't be able to hold her hand because he'd be spending quality time alone in another room doing his business into a steel dish without romantic candlelight or a Bee Gees soundtrack.

"So what do we really think about Shane Tyler?" she

said.

"I tried," said Kay.

"You tried?" Cathy was puzzled.

"Yes, I tried and I failed. With Shane Tyler. All I'll say is it was fun. Please don't ask for details."

"Oh…" said Cathy.

"I'd like details," said Grace.

"It's over," said Kay, "but here are the edited highlights…"

An hour later, Cathy and Kay saw Grace safely home.

"Fancy helping me find my ancestor?" Cathy said as they neared their own homes.

A moment later, Cathy let them in.

"Chris? You there?" she called.

There was no reply. Then her phone pinged. It wasn't Chris, though – it was an IVF clinic reminder.

"He must have popped out," she said. "Fancy some tea, Kay?"

Kay was soon comfortably seated in the lounge while Cathy sorted out the tea in the kitchen.

The front door opened.

"Hello Cath," said Chris, coming in and spying his wife in the kitchen. "Just been in with Roland. He's given me a biriyani recipe. Oh, and the IVF clinic texted…"

At this point, Chris glanced into the lounge where Kay was looking up at him from the sofa.

"Ah…" he managed to say.

He left the room and made a thing about grabbing a shower, even though Cathy new he'd already had one.

A few moments later, she sat with Kay in the lounge, sipped her tea and said, "So, I expect you heard that?"

"I never heard a thing, Cath. If that's what you'd

prefer."

Cathy sighed. Then she put her tea down.

"He's an oaf, but it's okay. To tell the truth, if I don't talk to someone, I'll explode. I've gone over it so many times with Chris, but we're running on empty now. I mean it's got to the stage where I avoid it. He sings in the shower, he hums happy tunes while he's getting his fishing stuff together, and... the last four frozen transfers I had all failed."

"That's awful," said Kay. "But you never know. Maybe next time?"

"We've got one embryo left from six we had frozen three years ago. I've been putting off going back to London to use it. I thought of trying for a job up here, but Chris knows my passion is history. If I take a job in an office, he'll know it's just to avoid London, where friends with babies and IVF treatment lurk. Even my sister's pregnant."

"Right."

"I've felt so happy here. No worrying, no stress."

"Then stay," said Kay. "Chris will just have to get used to it."

"That's the thing. Chris would support me if I took an admin job, but that's not fair. He wants to be a dad."

"Perhaps we could find another way to persuade Shane Tyler to keep the castle open then. Chris would understand that passion for history outweighing the other one. Besides, I'd imagine the IVF is expensive."

"The first three rounds were free on the NHS. Since then it's been five grand a go. The thing is I'd pay fifty grand if I knew it would be successful. Not that we have fifty grand. Not unless we sold our home in Finchley, and we'd never do that."

"I suppose the optimism lessens each time," said Kay.

"You're not kidding. The first time we were so excited. You block out the fact they turn you into a medical experiment with check-ups and medication to prepare the womb, and endless people gawping. Some days I feel so much for Chris, because his side of the equation is all systems go."

Kay shook her head. "From what I've come to know of Chris, he's the last man on earth who would think about blame."

"I know he's desperate to become a dad though. I know he hurts inside."

"So London isn't just about work…"

"No, London is about friends who have seen something IVF-related on the internet. You know, the vital missing piece of info that will change our lives, even though we've searched through every scrap of knowledge out there."

"I know this isn't what you want to hear," said Kay, "but don't give up. Unless your uterus explodes, don't throw in the towel."

Cathy laughed, although her mirth died away a little too quickly.

"My ovaries swell up. That's it. My only hope is another round of being rendered unconscious and have my innards scraped… and then enduring weeks of medication including pessaries up the tunnel of love, meaning hellfire thrush, nausea, headaches, fatigue, bloating, sweating, dizziness and cramps – with Chris on notice that if he even looks at me in that way he'll get my knee in his groin."

"It sounds the best possible fun," said Kay. "I can't believe you don't want to go through it again."

"Some cycles give me so much pain I can only crawl to the loo. And then then there's the bit where I start to think I'm pregnant, because all the signs are there. And then I'm re-evaluating my avoidance strategy for the baby aisle at the supermarket…"

"So will you try again?" said Kay.

Cathy fell silent. It wasn't an easy question to answer.

"I can take all the indignities that come with it… but that week and a half after they've put the embryo in… that's a long time to wait for the test to confirm if I'm pregnant. They say get on with a normal life, but every single second of every day and night is focused on one thing. I've had four transfers…"

Kay took a sip of tea but this time said nothing.

"It's the hope that hurts most, Kay."

Kay put her cup down.

"There is a bright side. I know he smells of fish and maggots sometimes, but you've got Chris."

"Chris? What that big oaf? That stupid dumb twit who has put up with all my crazy moods, my crying, who's been there alongside me at all those appointments, brought me a cup of tea when he's noticed I'm lost, who says he loves me, however nutty I get…"

Cathy's phone pinged. She checked in case it was an apologetic Chris texting from upstairs. It wasn't – it was Shane Tyler.

Cathy composed herself before relating the contents to Kay.

"Mr Tyler says he's had the local press onto him asking for his reaction to the protest. He wants to know what the hell's going on."

"Right… I can't see him changing his mind," said Kay. "I think we have to accept the castle's going to shut down for a year. I think your decision is more about going back to London or staying here in a new job."

"Unless we can persuade him to keep it open while we

work around the builders."

"I think we're in danger of going around in circles," said Kay. "How about we take a break from the castle and try to find your Mr Barrett-Barnett?"

"Yeah, okay…"

Cathy fired up the laptop and they were soon looking at Frederick Barrett in the 1861 census."

"Right," said Kay. "The 1851 census, Frederick Barnett…"

It didn't take long to find nine-year-old Frederick Barrett under his incorrectly transcribed name in the database. They clicked through to the original handwritten entry and squinted.

"The handwriting looks like a seismograph," said Kay. "You can see how Barrett could be added to the searchable records as Barnett."

"Definitely," said Cathy, "especially to some poor so-and-so transcribing zillions of squiggly names."

The interesting thing for Cathy was finally meeting Frederick's parents, Alfred and Eliza Barnett – or Barrett.

"Oh look," said Kay. "They lived in the Queen's Arms public house in Field Way, Castle Hill."

"A pub?" said Cathy. "Is it still there?"

Kay shook her head. "I've lived here my whole life and I've never heard of the Queen's Arms *or* Field Way."

Cathy googled the pub but it didn't exist.

She tried searching for Field Way.

That didn't exist either.

A lost pub in a missing street?

Cathy's phone rang. It was Chris.

"Hi, lovely hubby upstairs. What's up?"

"Eh? Oh… I was just wondering about lunch."

Cathy cut straight to telling him what they had just discovered – only she ended the call looking puzzled.

"What's up?" Kay asked.

"It's just Chris being strange. As you heard, I told him about the lost pub."

"What did he say?"

"If I can remember rightly, he said 'ha-ha-ha-ha, I might have an answer for you. No, it can't be. Ha-ha-ha-ha.'"

18

Here's An Idea

Having completed a copywriting task for a client, Chris was enjoying an afternoon session on the canal – not fishing, but helping a few of the regular volunteers tidy and restore a section of tow-path farther out into the countryside. Over the years, the concrete slopes leading to a foot bridge had eroded and broken up. There was also a bramble invasion making a natural path on the far side of the canal impossible to use.

Chris wondered – was this another example of him committing a little more to Castle Hill? Or simply a matter of being helpful?

He was mixing concrete in a large bucket for a man called Dean, who had brought his boisterous nine- and eleven-year-old daughters to keep them engaged and screen-free for at least some of the school holidays.

Vic was there too, watching and advising, whether advice was needed or not.

While they were working, a very smart narrow boat

pulled up. With red and pink roses painted onto black gloss, along with shiny brass fittings, it was owned by a retired couple from Birmingham called Harry and Josie. Within the hour, Chris had enjoyed a cup of tea and several choc 'n' nut cookies with them, learned everything about Harry's former life as a building control officer at a local council, Josie's long years at a big insurance firm, all about their grown-up son and daughter, all about where they'd been on the boat, the Daisy-Mae, and where they were headed to next.

"Do you have a fridge in there to keep your beer cold?" he asked.

"We do," said Josie.

Chris's desire to own a narrow boat ramped up a notch.

Naturally, it was hard for Harry and Josie to leave. The engine was in good order and the rest of their day had been mapped out, but they just couldn't seem to pull free of Vic, who had only got as far as 1948.

"The idea was to close most of our smaller waterways, but it wasn't so simple. Each canal required separate legislation. Of course, that didn't stop the Government cutting all remaining funding."

"Fascinating," said Harry.

"Well, naturally, Tom Rolt wasn't going to lie down. In 1950, he planned a national rally of boats at Market Harborough. It was going to be a protest at the way the government was ignoring the working boats of Britain. The strange thing was... Robert Aickman didn't agree."

"Oh?" said Chris. Although, he was busy mixing sharp sand ballast with cement, he found Vic's history lesson helped with the monotony of the task.

"Not that Mr Aickman didn't want to see the boats coming together," said Vic. "It's just he wasn't so troubled by the passing of the commercial life of the canals. He was more looking to the future – you know, saving the canals for good people such as Harry and Josie here."

"There you go, guys," said Chris. "He was doing it for you."

"So what happened?" asked Harry.

"Well, Robert Aickman turned Market Harborough into a people's festival with a grand pageant, marquees and stalls, films and shows, beer and food… I swear to you on my life, there were boats lined up for miles out of town, the tow-paths were crammed full… and, well, at least fifty thousand people flocked to the place."

"Impressive," said Josie.

"Yes," said Vic, "but Tom Rolt didn't like that at all. While he wanted to save the working boats and commercial routes, Aickman came up with the idea of saving every single mile of canal for the people. He said the festival proved there was a public appetite for boats and that they wanted the canals to mean fun and relaxation for everyone. Guess who came out on top?"

"Aickman?" Josie ventured.

"Correct. In 1952, Mr Rolt was expelled from the Inland Waterways Association. And do you know what happened next?"

"He's gonna tell us," muttered Dean.

"The IWA membership took off. It started to grow into a movement that would change Britain. At least in canal usage terms."

"Thank God people fought for the canals," said Josie.

"It's been brilliant," said Harry, "but we really ought to be going. We have a destination to reach before it gets dark."

Harry and Josie finally bade the volunteers farewell

and set off for a place to finish the day and spend the night.

That was Chris's cue to take the wheelbarrow to retrieve more ballast from Dean's open-back truck, which was parked on the road beyond a strip of scrubland.

Caroline went with him to 'stretch her legs'.

"Dean's kids are well-behaved, aren't they," she said.

"Yes, they are," said Chris.

"It must be wonderful to be around young minds. They're like sponges, waiting to soak up all kinds of learning."

"Yes, I expect they'll know everything about the history of the canals before long."

"Oh, Vic doesn't mean to go on and on. He just worries there'll be no-one after him to share the history that's all around us."

"There's always someone ready to tell you the history of something," said Chris. "It's one of life's rules. You go anywhere and look at something and someone will come up to you and start telling you its history."

Caroline laughed a little.

"Imagine if you had kids, Chris. They'd get it twice over – you going on about the canals and Cathy with that castle of hers."

"Well, I don't know about that..."

· Chris had a vague urge to tell Caroline how he and Cathy wanted to become parents, but he feared she'd say something like 'there's treatment you can get, isn't there?' And Chris would have to say yes, there are one or two things you can try...

...but his heart ached for Cathy. One or two things? The daily medication, the umpteen appointments, the endless blood tests, scans, and indignities. And then the waiting...

As far as Chris was concerned, you could call Cathy a lot of things – some of them rude. But she was staunch and loyal, feisty and fair, a good listener, a great friend, and the top-top-toppest partner you could ever hope to have. She was many, many things to many, many people but she'd never be the one, single, sole thing she needed to make her life whole.

So he didn't tell Caroline.

Instead he loaded two large bags of ballast into the wheelbarrow.

"What's your view on collectibles?" he asked.

"How do you mean?"

Chris explained his idea of buying and selling old toy cars.

"You're sure you're not buying back into a lost youth?"

Chris thought back to his youth. He'd be doing it for a different reason – so that Cathy would see a man embracing his passions to make a better life for them.

But it wasn't really a passion.

"No, I'm probably not going through with it. I'm just…"

Looking for something.

He supposed he would give up and get back to doing what he'd always done – supporting Cathy.

"So, witchcraft," he said as they set off back to the canal. "I can't say I believe in it."

"We don't mean any harm, Chris. We're not really witches. We don't do magic spells or summon up demons. We just try to work for the good of all."

"Yeah, nothing wrong with that, I suppose."

"We follow a moral code but we don't preach. We're one with nature, connected to the universe, aware of the power we have to change our lives…"

"I'll say one thing," said Chris. "It's true sometimes when I'm at the waterside, it feels magic."

"There's a lot magic around water. Especially in moonlight. Ask for what you need. You'll be surprised."

"Yeah right. A lottery win."

"That might not be what you need."

Chris came to a halt.

"You think things can be influenced?"

"Earth is a crucible. Anything and everything can be influenced. That's earth's purpose. To give. All you need do is ask."

"Sorry, Caroline, I'm not a believer."

Chris pushed on again. Caroline followed.

"It's not compulsory," she said.

"I'm serious. People like you get ordinary people turning away from science and relying on nonsense."

"I would never advise anyone to turn away from science or medicine. What we offer is another way of seeing the world. Another way of engaging with a universe that is awaiting our communication. We don't brainwash people into anything."

"No, well, ignore me. I didn't mean to be rude."

They were almost at the canal-side.

"Good luck with it then, Chris," said Caroline.

"With what?"

"With whatever's troubling you."

Chris kept his focus on Vic, who was in full flow.

"…and the arguments went on between them. Having such differing views, they were never really going to fully agree."

"Sorry, Vic," said Chris, "who are we talking about?"

"Robert Aickman… the arguments he and Tom Rolt had after Aickman turned Tom's 1950 working boats rally into a people's festival."

"Oh right. Yes, you mentioned that earlier. It sounds like…" But Chris stopped dead. "Actually, it sounds like just the thing we're looking for."

19

The People's Festival

It was ten a.m. and Chris was first at the canal. The weather was fine and the breeze gentle, with plenty of sunshine and rising temperatures predicted for the next few days. In the distance, beyond the bridge, he could see Dave's boat, the Mary-Lou, making its way towards him.

Chris accepted he wouldn't find a way to enact a passion that didn't exist – but back in his regular role of supporting Cathy, he felt confident.

In short, Shane Tyler had agreed to pop over at three p.m. to see the boats gathering, so there was plenty of time for preparation work beforehand. Chris had told Dave and the others this would be about getting Tyler to pay for new lock gates so that they could begin the reclamation of the canal arm that ran along to the lost pub and beyond. This fitted in nicely with his ulterior motive – that of befriending Tyler in order to get him to accept Cathy's idea of keeping the castle open while the renovation work went on.

Dave and Sam aboard the Mary-Lou were soon alongside and, not long after, a team of volunteers had assembled.

"Right," said Dave. "We need the bottom gate patched up and closed tight."

He was indicating the gate between the lock chamber and the overgrown jungle that occupied the space where water would hopefully one day flow. This stretch of disused canal went through lower-lying land, hence the need for a lock to lower a boat coming from the main canal or to raise one heading the other way.

"We'll need to look at the ground paddle winding gear," said Sam. "It's seized up."

Chris nodded, grateful for the one cruising holiday break he'd taken all those years ago. He knew that the ground paddle was a kind of small trap door that let water in when you opened it using the winding gear on the lock-side.

"Once the bottom gate is secure, we'll check out the top gate," said Dave.

All eyes turned to the gate between the lock chamber and the higher level main canal. This gate had two paddles or trap doors – one in the upper part of the gate and one in the ground.

"Once we're happy, we'll bring the Mary-Lou through," said Sam.

Chris felt the tension build. The lock hadn't been used in years. It was his idea to put the Mary-Lou in the chamber, but it was Dave's boat. He didn't want anything to go wrong.

"Once the Mary-Lou is in place," said Chris, "the other boats will rally to this point on the main canal. Then, aboard the Mary-Lou, I'll give the speech."

"Let's hope Vic didn't write it for you," Dean

muttered.

Chris glanced across to Vic, who was busy extracting a pack of mints from his tweed jacket pocket and seemingly hadn't heard.

"Have you got your costume?" asked Sam.

"It's in my kit bag," said Chris, still not too sure whether dressing up would look brilliant or not.

He enjoyed the next few hours of hard graft. The main thing was cutting and fitting boards over parts of the lower gate and freeing up all the winding gear. At the end of it all, the winding gears were operative, but the bottom lock gate repairs looked decidedly temporary.

Next it was time to fill the lock. Chris was handed a key and tasked with operating the winding gear on the lock-side. Turning the handle would release water from the main canal through the ground paddle trap door into the lock chamber.

"Here goes…"

He turned the handle over and over, recalling how to do so from his Norfolk Broads boating holiday of long ago. Soon, water began to flow into the chamber and the mood among the volunteers noticeably lifted. This was genuine progress. Even Vic was speechless.

Once the lock was half full, Dave opened the paddle in the upper gate to let even more water cascade in. It was like filling the world's biggest bath tub.

Once the water in the lock reached the same height as the main canal, volunteers pushed open the top gate to allow the Mary-Lou to enter.

As she moved inside, the small crowd broke into applause.

"God bless all who pass through," said Vic.

As soon as the Mary-Lou was snugly inside, the gate was closed.

Chris checked his watch. It was almost time.

They had eight boats in all. Twenty boat-owners had expressed support but wouldn't be able to get there in time. This was fine though. Tyler would still be impressed with a mini people's festival of boats.

Chris grabbed his bag and made his way aboard the narrow boat. Vic followed him, even into the cabin.

"Did I tell you about Robert Aickman's 'save every mile' campaign?"

"Yes, Vic, you did," said Chris, removing his trousers.

"The British Transport Commission, which by then governed most canals, rejected it. They had no interest in developing amenities for tourism, see?"

"Not very visionary, were they."

"They decided to close the whole lot. The end of the canals. Can you imagine it?"

"No, even I would have been angry about that," said Chris, removing his rugby shirt.

"Well, we were lucky. As I might have mentioned, back in the Victorian era, each new canal had to be approved by a separate Act of Parliament. That gave volunteers the chance to fight for each canal as the British Transport Commission targeted it for closure. While they would prepare to steer the repeal of the relevant act through Parliament, volunteers could get a campaign underway."

"Yes, I see..."

Chris began buttoning up his white shirt.

"One way the commission would try to close a canal was to insist it had become unnavigable, and therefore useless. That led to campaigners from the Inland Waterways Association flocking to that canal in a mass cruise to take up their legal right of navigation. No word of a lie, Chris – it turned into a decade of conflict between ordinary people and the authorities."

"It's hard to believe it could come to that, Vic," said Chris, fixing a cravat around his collar.

"When they tried to close the Kennet and Avon Canal, our people signed up thirty sympathetic MPs as honorary members of the IWA. That held things up for a bit. Not so with the other big campaign. We lost the Stroudwater Canal in Parliament, although we had 112 MPs vote against closure."

"There's certainly more to it than most people understand."

"That's true. In 1955, the enemy – that's the government, Chris – they identified 770 miles of waterway they wanted to close."

"Okay, you win, Vic. That is ridiculous. Who did these officials think they were?"

"They tried to close the Huddersfield Narrow Canal, Chris, but opinions were changing fast. Petitions were signed. People spoke out. When the Commission tried to get it into Parliamentary business, it wasn't chosen."

"Good," said Chris, pulling on a pair of black trousers.

"Then the campaign to save the Kennet and Avon Canal got going at full steam. A petition bearing 22,000 signatures was brought up to London from Bristol by water, despite parts of the silted-up canal having to be negotiated by canoe to get through."

"Did it work?" asked Chris, pulling on his slip-on shoes. "No, what am I saying. Even I know it's one of the best-known canals in England."

"Yes, it worked," said Vic, following Chris out onto the deck. "Our people defeated the enemy in Parliament. The Bill to close the canal was thrown out."

"Great work, Vic," said Chris, pulling on his hired costume Victorian coat. "I bet you wish you'd been born earlier so you could have been there."

"You're not wrong, Chris, but the fight wasn't over. Next came Stourbridge – and I *was* there. To be at Stourbridge... it was like being at the Battle of Agincourt. Without the blood and carnage, obviously."

"Speaking of blood and carnage," said Chris, donning his stove-pipe hat. He'd spotted Cathy approaching. "Ahoy there!"

"Thought I'd lend some support," Cathy said before saying hello to all those gathered.

"Mr Tyler should be along soon," said Chris.

"That's what I was hoping."

"Please don't throw him in the water, Cath."

That raised a laugh from the crowd.

"Why's he dressed like Abraham Lincoln?" said a young boy in the crowd.

"I'm attempting to look like Isambard Kingdom Brunel," said Chris, "although, between you and me, I'm not sure he had anything to do with canals."

"We've got a bit of leakage through the bottom gate," said Dave.

"I knew we should have persuaded Caroline to leave work early," said volunteer Liz. "An unblessed enterprise lacks harmony."

"Let's hope this gets underway soon," said Dave, "Best nudge open that paddle in the top gate. Let a bit more water in."

On the lock-side, Sam said hello to Cathy.

"What's going to happen when you leave?" she asked in typical direct fashion.

"We don't know for sure I'll be leaving."

"In my experience, big money usually wins."

Cathy took into the face of a confident eight-year-old girl who seemed to have a decent grasp of how the world worked.

"I probably can't teach you much, Sam, but please take this one piece of advice on board. Never bow down to big money. It's not always in the right."

"Dad says the castle needs a lot of money spent on it. I've seen the big crack in the arch."

"Yes, it does need money. The crack is only part of it. Are you a regular visitor?"

"In the summer, if I can get mum or dad to take me. I like the mediaeval weapons and I also like the view from the top of the keep. It's like being in charge of Castle Hill."

"Yes, you get the feeling you can boss all the peasants about from up there."

"It's a shame you're not needed."

"Yes... it *is* a shame."

That hurt coming from a child.

Just then, Shane Tyler arrived and joined the throng standing back from the lock to take in the spectacle of Chris posing as a Victorian character.

"Is Chris good at speeches?" Sam asked.

Cathy shrugged. "We'll soon find out."

"I thought your education protest was nuts," said Tyler.

"Oh, Mr Tyler, I didn't see you there," said Cathy. "Did you come down the tow-path or walk straight across the water?"

"The canals of Britain," Chris began from the deck of the boat, "were cut through hard ground by men with picks and shovels."

Cathy turned again to Shane Tyler.

"Children have a right to visit the castle this summer."

"Getting kids to pose like that was underhand."

"This would have been during the Industrial Revolution," Chris pronounced.

A flash went off. It was a local newspaper photographer.

From the boat, Chris tried to ignore the photographer. He also tried to ignore what appeared to be an argument between Cathy and Shane Tyler standing either side of bemused-looking canal volunteer Liz. Her comment came back to him, about Caroline bringing harmony. It was certainly in short supply.

"The community comes first in Castle Hill," said Cathy.

"The community will gain a world class attraction."

Chris decided to press on.

"The idea, during the Industrial Revolution, was to have an effective means of transporting timber, coal, grain and so on."

"The castle doesn't need to close."

"The answer was to create the highways of the Victorian Age – on water."

"Yes, it does – for twelve months."

"The barges and boats were able to transport goods and supplies…" Chris wondered – was Dave getting taller? "…on what became an ever-growing network."

"There's more water leaking through the bottom gate," said Dave.

"Today, we still have our canals thanks to the efforts of the Inland Waterways people…"

"You're going down," said Sam in a stage whisper.

"…who took on the authorities to save…"

"You're being unreasonable."

"So are you!"

Chris stood on tiptoes. "...to save them. Today, the sight of a narrow boat is enough to raise one's spirits." *If not the water level.*

He was aware that Cathy, Shane Tyler, and all those gathered were also on tiptoes, peering over the edge of the lock to see the top of his stove pipe hat disappearing.

"The show's over, folks," said Dave. "Someone open that top gate paddle and let some water in."

Chris was disappointed. He hadn't got to his rousing finale, which meant Shane Tyler probably wouldn't be impressed.

Or was a re-think in order?

Yes, he would try again, only next time it would probably be worth thinking smaller.

20

The Lure

Once Chris had helped Dave to rescue the Mary-Lou from the lock, he joined him aboard to enjoy the short ride to a spot twenty yards along the main canal.

"Sorry about that, Dave," he said for the tenth time. "I don't know what I was thinking."

"You were thinking it might help us get the lock repaired," said Dave. "That justifies giving a bad speech in a funny costume."

"Thanks," said Chris, knowing that to be only half the story. He very much needed to build a bridge to Shane Tyler in order to win him over to Cathy's way of seeing things.

"Some people might think you're a bit weird," said Sam, coming along the tow-path with Liz, "but I think you're a canal hero."

"Really?"

"It's not your fault Cathy started a fight."

"Yes, well, she was very keen to get her point of view

across."

Sam waved them goodbye and went off with Liz who was going to see her home.

"Beer, Chris?" said Dave.

"Mind-reader."

A happy hour or two later, with the sun setting, Chris stepped off the Mary-Lou onto the tow-path with his kit bag over his shoulder.

"Thanks Dave. Don't worry, we'll get Tyler next time."

"Yeah, take care, Chris."

Chris watched the Mary-Lou ease her way under the bridge towards her mooring just before the town. He wasn't ready to go straight home though. There was too much going on in his head, and he could think better when walking.

One thing uppermost in his mind was how to coax Shane Tyler back to the canal. He just needed one final crack at him. Once won over, Tyler would pay up for the lock repairs and come around to seeing Cathy's point of view.

So what was the plan? How could he lure Tyler back?

What do I like?

He stopped. Could it be that simple? Just have a beer on a boat?

He laughed.

Yes, Tyler would like that.

Chris reached the scene of his earlier failure. The lock chamber was empty once again with its erstwhile contents having leaked through the bottom gate to aid the jungle growing on the disused canal.

He tried to picture it in full working order. A boat…

his own boat... moving though the open bottom gate into the canal that would have him glide past the lost pub... only it would be the found pub by then. He'd pull up at a suitable mooring, hop off, and head for the bar. Yes, an ice cold lager in the beer garden, a glass of prosecco for Cathy, a view of their boat, of the sun glinting on the water, of a brighter future.

He pushed through the buddleia and bramble.

"Oww, flippin' killer plants..."

He pushed into the dense bush, stopping every twelve inches to pull branches away from his face. Every other twelve inches, he had to prevent one from piercing his groin. The tow-path underfoot was narrow and it would be easy to step off and drop into deep jungle.

It was slow progress, especially with his kit bag continually snagging.

Five minutes and a few yards in, he felt as if he might be in the middle of the rainforest. It wouldn't have surprised him to see an Amazonian tribe coming the other way.

More than once, he had to double back as the trunks of these bushes were almost tree-like and unwilling to bend out of the way.

Ten minutes in, he tripped and banged his knee – but he continued on, refusing to give up. There was a pub out there somewhere and he intended to find it.

And then...

He was into clearer ground. Ahead stood a two-tier structure. The lost pub! And he was entering its long-abandoned beer garden.

He got up close to a window and tried to peer inside. It appeared to have been decaying for some considerable time. It was so quiet. So very quiet. And so very, very deserted. As if no-one had been there for—

"CHRIS!"

"Arggghhh!!!"

"I sometimes come here imagining the canal full of water and Tom and Angela Rolt coming along in Cressy."

"Vic... one degree scarier and I'd have been meeting Tom and Angela in the bloody afterlife!"

A car went by somewhere farther back.

"There's a road...?"

"Yes, there's a path up to it. How else do you think I got here?"

"Hang on, the lost pub has a path... to a road...?"

"The old road. It's hardly used but it goes down to the where the old factories were. Nothing much there now, of course."

Chris ventured to the edge of the building and stared in disbelief along the clear sixty-foot path leading to the road.

"Well, I'll be..."

He returned to the decrepit beer garden. Before sitting down on a bench, he checked it for sturdiness.

"Don't want to end up in a viral video."

"A what?"

Chris guessed that Vic wasn't into viral videos.

"So, Tom and Angela aboard Cressy," he said. "Yes, it would be quite a sight."

"Boats are in the blood, Chris. Every people on earth has a history involving boats. Canals, rivers, lakes, oceans..."

"Yes, strange how boats can affect so much. Cathy was telling me about the White Ship. You heard about that, Vic?"

"No, I can't say I have."

"It was a ship that went down and caused a civil war."

"Boats can do that," said Vic.

"Imagine it. One boat starting all that trouble."

"Imagine one boat saving all our canals."

"Yeah... boats, eh? Shame we haven't got a beer to toast them."

"Yes, it's just history now. I often think how much it's all around us. Every street we walk down, every canal we navigate, every road we travel. A thousand events have happened wherever we turn. Some important, most not so..."

"Yes, history is certainly all around us, Vic. You know the pub from the old days then, do you?"

"Oh yes, a lovely pub it was. Very convivial. And the landlord wasn't too quick to chuck you out at night, if you know what I mean. I'm going back forty years, of course."

Chris quite liked it. With a bit of vision... okay, a lot of vision, it was possible to see the pub as a real asset to the area. A great pub, serving great beer, wine and food... yes, food... great food... right on the waterfront. Okay, so you needed to stretch the vision to include clearing the canal of half a rainforest...

The vision faded, but it didn't completely die away. It was too poetic for that.

The Lost Pub...

Chris imagined those words on a big sign fixed to the side of the building. What if he tried to lure Cathy into switching her passion from a crumbling old castle to this fine potential pub? No doubt she would gladly... gladly... punch him on the nose.

But the vision still wasn't finished. What if he could get Shane Tyler involved? The pub would be a Cathy and Chris business venture, but... yes, something more could come of it. Something substantial situated just along from the pub. Something that would put this part of

Leicestershire on the map.

An idea was beginning to take shape in Christopher Chappell's head.

An all-new big idea.

21

Waterside

Late, the following afternoon, the sun was out, the temperature was rising, and Cathy was heading into town to do a bit of shopping. With Chris doing a spot of fishing while waiting for a client to get back to him, it was a useful distraction from the business of the castle.

Seeing Shane Tyler's car roll by didn't cloud her mood. She wasn't going to let him spoil her day. Although...

She watched the car pull up just past the church.

Tyler got out and crossed the road by the bridge. He was heading for the canal.

Why?

Chris was down there fishing. He hadn't said a word about meeting Tyler again. What was going on?

It occurred to Cathy that there was only one way to find out.

Two minutes later, she was in the bushes watching Tyler getting friendly with Chris aboard the Mary-Lou.

He must have borrowed it off Dave. What's he up to?

She needed to get closer in order to eavesdrop. Of course, that would be nuts but she simply couldn't think of another way to get the information she needed. So, on hands and knees, she crawled through the bushes until she was close enough to hear them.

Unbelievably, Chris had opened a couple of beers and there they were, two blokes, standing by the steering wheel, drinking and looking like best mates.

"Yeah, I was in the Americas Cup," Tyler was saying. He went on, at length, to describe the adrenalin rush of competing in an ocean yacht race. Cathy almost dozed off. When she refocused, Chris was explaining how a group of canal locks taking you uphill or downhill is called a flight – unless they're joined together, with the bottom gate of one lock being the top gate of the next. Then it's a staircase. For reasons Cathy couldn't fathom, he followed this dull piece of information with some key features of the Waterways Code. Maximum speed 4 mph. Never create a breaking wash. Always have buoyancy aides for kids. Fire equipment. Pass other boats on the right wherever possible.

With Tyler managing to stay awake through that lot, Chris went into a eulogy concerning the types of bridge you might encounter on the canal. Namely, the swing bridge and the lifting bridge.

"What's your winning argument, Chris?" Tyler asked.

"You never spill your beer."

Cathy shook her head, but incredibly Tyler laughed.

"I've also had a bit of an idea," said Chris. "A big one, to be fair. An all-new big idea."

"Go on," said Tyler.

"Okay, imagine this. New lock gates would mean we can clear the old canal arm that goes down to where the old factories were. The idea is that you buy up one of the sites canal-side and dig out a narrow boat marina."

"A marina? Interesting."

Cathy couldn't get her head around Chris's all-new big idea. Where the hell had that come from? Was he even serious?

"Go on," said Tyler.

"Okay, so you put in a new building to house a store for spares and repairs, plus provisions… you put in bicycle hire, a gym, shower facilities, and a restaurant. Then, next door, me and Cathy reopen the lost pub."

Cathy's eyes almost popped out of her head. What was her husband drinking? Battery acid?

"Obviously, we'd do a different line of hot food from your restaurant," said Chris. "You know, to give people a choice. We'd both draw in plenty of customers from the town, plus we'd have tourists and boat people looking for an overnight or short stay."

Cathy was still trying to take it all in.

"So you reckon we'd both be winners?" said Tyler.

"Yes, and we'd both have somewhere to moor our narrow boats."

"Who said anything about me buying a narrow boat?" said Tyler.

Cathy nodded. *At last, someone speaks for me!*

"Oh, you'll want a boat, Shane. Seriously, you will."

Tyler looked around and exhaled a short breath.

"Right, I'm going to say no, Chris. I like your thinking, but it's not for me. Why don't you raise the finance and carry it out yourself?"

"Yes, well… we'll see."

"Look, I have to go. I have a meeting with an architect. Keep in touch, yeah?"

"Yeah… will do."

Cathy backed herself further into the thick bushes as

Tyler jumped onto the tow-path and headed off.

Her phone rang.

It was Chris.

"Hi Cath – got a minute?"

Wedged tight, Cathy moved slightly to prevent a sharp, stubby branch ripping out her throat.

"Chris, I'm in the middle of something, but go on…"

"It's about Tyler. I chatted to him about investing in the canal."

"Oh?"

"Well, there's now a man in town who wants to become part of the narrow boat community. On the downside, it's not Tyler, it's me."

"Oh Chris. Fat lot of good, you are!"

A few minutes later, while Chris imagined owning his own boat, he spotted Dave coming along the tow-path.

"Any luck?" Dave called.

"Not yet. He'll crack though."

Dave climbed aboard.

"What if he doesn't?"

"You mean what if the ol' Chris Chappell psychology-magic doesn't take hold? Well, that would probably mean Cathy and me going back to London."

"We'd be sorry to see you go. The pair of you have been good for this community."

"Thanks Dave, but Cathy's got a good career in London with British Heritage."

"Of course."

"She loves it up here though…"

Chris didn't mention how Cathy was keen to avoid facing IVF in London. Men didn't talk about things like that.

"Well, I'll be off then," said Dave. "Unless you need a ride?"

"No, I'm good, thanks. I'll see you soon."

Chris hopped off and gave the Mary-Lou a push to help Dave get her away from the bank.

"There's a boat for sale up near my mooring," said Dave. "Looks decent."

"I might take a look later," said Chris. "I want to catch up with Cathy first. Oh, there she is in the bushes, spying on us."

Cathy and Chris were strolling along the tow-path away from Castle Hill. By now, the early evening weather was stunning, with birdsong in the air and the waters of the canal utterly still unless disturbed by the occasional passing boat.

"I still can't believe you gave me away to Dave," said Cathy.

"He's a senior police detective, Cath. I'm sure he would have spotted you."

"A woman is perfectly entitled to hide in bushes to spy on people without her husband making a fuss about it."

"Well, that's all done. We're just winding down now, relieving the stress, letting nature restore our equilibrium, and burning off a few calories."

"Yes, well, we still have the Tyler problem – in case you'd forgotten."

"There is no Tyler problem, Cath. He's a wealthy man who wants to restore the castle to its former glory. No-one is massively bothered about it closing down for a year. No-one apart from you, that is. And I know why, and I just want you to know we can become a different kind of couple."

"Now you're burbling, Chris. I don't understand a word you're saying."

"Sure you do. I'm saying we can become one of those professional couples who are so focused on their careers they forget to have kids. We can join them in shrugging it off as unimportant."

"And where would we live as this professional couple?"

"In London."

"Right. You've thought this through, haven't you."

"A bit, yes."

"I don't want to go back to London."

"You need to accept our situation. Not right away, and not over the next week or two, but eventually. You need to see yourself a year or two from now being happy working for British Heritage in London."

"And that's it?"

"No, that's not it. After a year or two... or three or four... we need to decide if we should adopt."

"Adopt?"

"Yes, if we can't have our own, we should consider it."

"Where's this coming from, Chris?"

"I don't know. My mind is usually calm and serene. Right now it's like a washing machine with a full load. There's all sorts of stuff churning about in there."

"Well, I *have* considered it. I've considered adoption *and* surrogacy a million times. It's our baby I want. It's our own baby I absolutely crave and feel cheated out of."

"I know."

"Do you?"

"Yes."

Cathy paused a moment. "Sorry... I know you do. And I know you mean well. And I know you're a good man. I also know you'd be the best dad in the world."

They fell silent and just enjoyed the feel of the earth beneath their feet and the sight of the sun dropping lower onto the horizon.

"I bumped into Caroline the other day," Chris eventually said.

"Oh? What was she up to?"

"Nothing. We just had a chat."

"What about?"

"Oh... nothing much."

"Then why are you telling me?"

"Oh because... well... did you know she's a witch?"

"You what?"

"A white witch."

"Caroline?"

"Yes."

"Caroline, who works for the police?"

"Yes, she's a witch. Not an evil one. A good one. And she's not actually called a witch."

"What exactly were you and Tyler drinking?"

"I'm being serious. Caroline says it's all about asking for what you want so the universe can provide it. She helps people with the process."

"I hope you're not suggesting we let her put a spell on us?"

"She doesn't seem dangerous or anything."

"Oh great. I'll book the train tickets for Hogwarts, shall I?"

"She doesn't have a wand, Cath."

"Chris, we'll always have days when we feel desperate. We just have to see it out."

"Forget I mentioned it. How about we just sit down and watch the sunset...?"

Cathy sighed, but followed Chris away from the deserted tow-path to a patch of dry grass. They sat in silence for half an hour, just holding hands, and then each other.

"Full moon rising," Chris said.

"Mmm."

"Reflecting off the water nicely."

"This is witch talk, isn't it."

"Of course it isn't."

"Yes it is."

"Alright, according to Caroline, there's magic around water… so… I suppose… if one… well, two, obviously – one would be weird… but if two people… well, the moon and the water… it's just about connecting and asking…"

"Are you suggesting what I think you're suggesting?"

"Yes, but with the proviso that all is lost. We're putting hope away so it doesn't torture us again. We can start by celebrating our new-found freedom."

"A moonlight flit?"

"Why not? Caroline might not pack a magic wand, but I do."

Cathy laughed for the first time in a while. Then, by the water, under the moon, she kissed her man.

22

Muniments

Times were dangerous. Holding on would be difficult. Resolve was vital amid the cut and thrust of others' dark ambition. Hugh de Gaul stopped for breath on the spot where, almost nine centuries later…

…Chris Chappell paused. He was thinking about getting started on his laptop. Finding more clients – that was the thing. The cut and thrust of business. After a nice walk in the morning sunshine?

Yes, why not freshen up the blood supply to the brain with a stroll before work. He could stop at the bakers while he was out.

He left the house and set off along Castle Close towards the High Street.

A few doors along, Grace was at her window. He waved. She waved back, but more in a 'stop right there' kind of way.

Chris waited while she came to the front door.

"Could you open my curtain, Chris? One side's stuck."

"Stand back, Grace. Curtain Man is here to do curtainly deeds. Where is the offending drape?"

Chris was soon tugging and pulling at a curtain at the back of the through-lounge.

"There! Thanks to Curtain Man, your full view of the garden is now restored."

"I don't suppose you're on speaking terms with Lightbulb Man?"

A moment later, Chris was wobbling on a chair to change a bulb in the kitchen. Then he hopped off and flicked the switch.

"There, Lightbulb Man's work is done."

"Not quite. There's the front half of the lounge. Let me make you something to eat. Fancy a bacon sandwich?"

"Ooh, a bacon sandwich sounds spot on, Grace."

"Well, you'll need it to keep all those superpowers topped up."

Chris held his hands up. "Okay, I admit it. I'm not really Lightbulb Man. I am in fact a lightbulb ninja. It was an extensive course. Seven years in the Himalayas…"

"Tea or coffee?" Grace said, cutting him off.

"Oh… tea please."

While he changed the bulb in the lounge, he noticed something unusual about the decorative plaster ceiling rose.

"This moulding… it's a flower like on those gravestones."

Grace came to the lounge door.

"It's a primrose. My great grandfather had this place built. He would have had that put up."

"It's a shame you can't find a link between you and the earlier lot, Grace."

"Those records were lost a long time ago. No use

worrying about it now. You've seen my family history boards. My family goes all the way back. That's all that matters to me. I'm not trying to win a competition. Obviously, it would be nice if I could find some evidence."

Chris took a photo of the plaster primrose, having half an idea in mind for later.

Once he'd finished his work and sandwich, he got back to his walk – where he bumped into Cathy's predecessor in the High Street.

"Still in Castle Hill then?" said Henry.

"Yes, we're not done yet."

"Does Cathy enjoy the endless fighting with Mr Tyler? I really can't see her winning."

"No, she hates dealing with Tyler. It's just her way of passing the day, Henry."

"Hmmm, he's a powerful man, if you know what I mean."

Chris frowned. "No, I don't know what you mean."

"Oh, I'm just saying power comes from passion. For Mr Tyler, I mean. Then you have Cathy, a passionate woman when it comes to history. It's like one of those movies."

"Is it?"

"Yes, you know, one of those romantic movies where there's a frisson whenever the two characters lock horns."

"I'm sure that doesn't apply to Cathy and Shane Tyler."

"There's a sliver of hate, but also so much passion for what they're trying to achieve. It's like they're only a heartbeat away from making love."

"That's my wife you're talking about!"

"No, I'm talking about the movie scenario. Cathy and Mr Tyler? No, I'm not suggesting anything there. God forbid."

"Cheerio, Henry. I've got things to do."

Keen to put some distance between himself and Henry, Chris walked straight through the High Street towards the canal. He paused at the church though. On a whim, he was soon at the grave of Grace's great, great, great, great, great grandfather – Josiah Lincoln, 1742 to 1799. Checking his phone, he could see the primrose motif on Grace's ceiling matched the eroded one on the gravestone.

He looked to the bridge. A few hundred yards on, towards the countryside, an arm of the canal connected it to the river. That's where the earliest part of the town, including the old town hall, had been built – and destroyed by the hurricane and flood.

He wondered.

Yes, so there had been the Great Storm of 1703, but he knew how rivers overflowed. It was rarely a tsunami, more a gradual rise until the water flowed over the banks and into a flood plain. In other words, there would have been time to move at least some of the town hall records upstairs.

Although… did the old town hall break apart in an instant or was it simply so badly damaged that it had to be abandoned?

That might have given officials time to rescue records.

He looked around. He was on higher ground. What if the 1703 vicar here at the church took in records during the Great Flood?

He entered the church and found the vicar with new parents discussing a christening.

Chris took a seat and waited.

Ten minutes later, he got to speak with the reverend.

"I don't expect you to recall the Great Storm of 1703, but I was wondering if there were any old town hall records going back to it."

"Have you tried the new town hall? Or the local library?"

"A genealogist friend of mine has. She's also gone through the parish records. I was just wondering if you might have anything tucked away?"

"I very much doubt it. From what I know of the Great Storm, the old town hall was a wooden structure that collapsed during a hurricane."

"Yes, that's what I've heard."

"Not collapsed as such," said a hidden voice.

Vic appeared from an alcove, hands thrust deep into a mustard cardigan.

"Ah, it's Mr Howard, one of my volunteers," said the reverend. "I'm guessing he'll have more information than me."

"Yes, I know Vic," said Chris. "I can't imagine why I didn't go straight to him in the first place."

"Well now, young Chris," said Vic, coming to join them. "From what I've learned over many years, the old town didn't collapse as such. It had a huge, tall brick chimney at one end – and that's what the hurricane brought down. It crashed through the building, smashing it to pieces. The mayor and others were able to save some documents, but where they ended up… who knows."

"So we don't know where they went?" said Chris.

"No."

"The thing is," Chris continued, "we're reasonably sure they weren't transferred to the replacement town hall they built years later. And they're not in the parish council archive or the local library."

"Yes, well, the church here has old records," said Vic, "but it's all CMB."

"CMB?"

"Christenings, marriages and burials," said the reverend. "You're welcome to look. Perhaps Vic could show you. I have a couple of visits to make."

A few minutes later, Chris was with Vic in a small room full of dusty old volumes.

"Every CMB going back to 1685, Chris."

"Do you have any other records though?"

"I can't say we do."

Chris wracked his brain. There had to be something more he could do. The idea of leaving empty handed so he could go back to writing boring emails to prospective clients would... be...

Emails... communication...

Something was bubbling up from the depths.

"Vic, what if... say... the bishop wrote to the vicar in 1700? Would that be thrown away?"

"Ah no, that would be kept at the office in the vicarage. That's not records, see – that's correspondence."

"And how far back does the correspondence go?"

"No idea. It's not within my remit as a church volunteer."

"Right."

"But Maisie Edwards is there right now. She'll let us take a peek."

Chris followed Vic out of the church and down the lane to the old vicarage.

"God, how old's this place?"

"The oldest part is Tudor. Most of the rest was added in 1695. That's the date on the corner stone over there."

He was pointing to a huge weathered white stone.

Chris felt he may have come to the right place.

Inside, Vic called out to Maisie, who emerged from the kitchen holding a mug of coffee.

"This is Chris," said Vic. "I'll let him explain."

Once Chris had explained what they were looking for, Maisie shook her head.

"You don't want correspondence. You want muniments."

"We've already done muniments," said Vic. "In the church."

"What are muniments?" asked Chris.

"Records," said Vic.

"I'm not talking about CMB," said Maisie. "We have a muniment room upstairs. Well, I say room. More like a cupboard."

"Sounds promising," said Chris.

He followed Maisie and Vic upstairs. On the upper floor landing, Maisie led them to a walk-in cupboard that housed a floor-to-ceiling wooden pigeon-hole shelving unit. Every compartment was stuffed with papers, folders, scrolls, envelopes…

"So this lot goes back a long way, does it?" Chris asked.

"Yes," said Maisie. "It's all sorts, really. Too much of a mess to sort out. There's everything from ecclesiastical correspondence to receipts for work carried out – some of them go back centuries."

"You'll need permission from the vicar to root through this lot," said Vic. "You start and I'll get him on his mobile phone."

"Tell him I'd like to bring in a local genealogist too, please."

*

Chris sneezed again. He'd spent half an hour sifting through old documents when Jasmine joined him. An hour on from her arrival, they were joined by the vicar and had since stopped for tea downstairs in the main reception room.

"Well," said Jasmine, "I'm quite satisfied that some of the records from the original town hall are in the muniment room upstairs. It's just a guess, but I'd say the records that survived the Great Storm were brought to the church for temporary safekeeping. Then, when the new town hall opened, those records were transferred there. However, it's clear some records got mixed up and were left behind."

"I suppose we really ought to have everything indexed," said the vicar unconvincingly.

Jasmine smiled. "I have a feeling many of your predecessors have said the exact same thing."

A further two-hour search took place after their tea break. This had almost brought them to lunchtime when Chris read something... and read it again.

And then read it aloud.

"This indenture, made in the reign of our sovereign Charles the Second, in the year of our Lord God one thousand six hundred and seventy seven, between Henry Lincoln and Jeremiah Dupris in consideration of the sum of..."

Chris looked up.

"Don't stop," said Jasmine.

He refocused on the document.

"...the sum of one pound sterling paid by Jeremiah Dupris into the hand of Henry Lincoln in full settlement of all monies pertaining to the transfer of title of De Gaul Castle..."

Vic whistled. "He bought it for a pound? Sounds like a

bargain."

"Not necessarily," said Jasmine. "A castle and its estate can be a money drain. It's not for anyone who just happened to have a pound. You'll see the same thing today in loss-making businesses. There would have been lots of responsibilities that sapped the purse of the owner. They should be on there, Chris."

Chris scanned it. "Yep, money to the church, provisions for horses, repair of homes, maintaining paths, and at least twenty other things. It looks like the owner was responsible for everything, including making sure the sun rose each morning and there was water in the river."

He handed the document to Jasmine, who shared it with the vicar, Vic and Maisie.

Chris was wondering whether to call Cathy with the news. But he guessed she might overreact. Perhaps he could approach Shane Tyler and gently present the information. If handled with care, Shane might want to take a step back from the castle and let someone else handle things for him.

He texted Tyler, saying it was urgent. A moment later, Shane Tyler texted back suggesting they meet in the castle car park right away.

Chris was waiting in the car park. How many heroes had stood here and faced death? Who were they? Where were their names recorded? He wondered if he'd go down as an unrecorded hero – one who prevented a war between Cathy and Shane Tyler by virtue of his detective work leading to a dusty muniments cupboard. Mind you, the prospect of a fresh war between himself and Cathy would be on the cards if he handled this badly.

"Sorry we couldn't meet inside," said Tyler as he

approached. "I've got restoration people in there who won't give me a minute's peace."

"That's okay, Shane. This won't take long. I've got a photocopy of a document I came across."

He handed it to Tyler, who squinted at the dense lettering.

"You can read it at your leisure, Shane. The main thing is it's an official record of your ancestor paying cash for the castle in 1677."

Shane looked up from the document.

"You what?"

"One pound, to be exact."

"A pound? That doesn't sound likely."

"Jasmine reckons you can't value a castle in those times without factoring in all the commitments that come with ownership."

"I see…"

"I'm sorry it's not the evidence you were looking for."

Tyler took a few moments to go through the details. Finally he sighed.

"I assume Henry Lincoln was part of the original family line?"

"We don't know. He might have bought it from the original family or maybe there was a whole string of different owners."

"Maybe Lincoln and Dupris were two parts of the original family – one side selling it to the other."

"Could be," said Chris, "although it's an incredibly detailed document. If they were related, there's plenty of opportunity on the page to say so."

"So Jeremiah Dupris bought the place for cash. Just like me."

"Two down, one to go," said Chris. "You can't realistically claim your family built the castle, and neither can Cathy. That leaves us with Grace Darling. Her family has always said their line goes all the way back."

"But she doesn't have any decisive evidence."

"No, she doesn't. Maybe we'll never find out. There's certainly nothing in the records we found."

Tyler looked up at the side of the keep.

"Do you think you'll take a step back from it now, Shane?"

"God no. I reckon a complete shutdown should be brought forward to right now."

"Right," said Chris, wondering how Cathy might react. Perhaps a quick phone call pledging 100% support for any plan she was hatching would help.

23

Inspiration Strikes

In bright, warm sunshine, Cathy made her way along the High Street in a good mood. It was a lovely idea of Chris's to have a picnic by the canal. Of course, the choice of location was no surprise – he practically lived there.

But no. He was a good man and spending a little time by the canal would be good for them both.

She felt the weight of her bag laden with sandwiches, chocolate, fruit, beer, and a bottle of Beaujolais.

The fight with Shane Tyler was in the balance, she felt. She just needed to keep up the pressure without coming across as a psycho. She felt sure she could make him see sense in keeping the castle open while the repairs took place. And she wanted to thank Chris for his 100% support. That was the thing with him – he would never let her down.

And if she lost out to Tyler's inflexibility?

Cathy had decided she would return to London and

raid their savings account to pay for a fifth and final round of IVF. She had no faith it would work, but not to try…?

Passing the church, she paused. The spire rose high into the blue. A bird swooped overhead. Who really knew what lay beyond the mortal realm?

She wondered. Could she involve a Higher Power?

If you can hear me, please give us a bit of help.

"Hello there, young lady."

Cathy's gaze dropped from the church spire to Grace leaving through the main door.

"Hello Grace. Been to pray, have we?"

"Yes and no. I volunteer once a week. How about you? Have you come to pray?"

"Now what would I pray for?"

"Sometimes, whatever we're facing in life, we need to find that little extra help. If you're not a believer, it's okay to call it luck."

"I don't think I'm blessed with luck."

"You're still young and there's still time."

"Has Kay been talking, by any chance?"

"Absolutely not. But you take Mrs Brewer. Fifteen years she and her husband were trying for a baby – then bam."

"Good for them."

"Well, not really – he grew up to be a right little rat."

"Ah."

"At one point, he was supplying cocaine to half the Midlands."

"Right."

"Enjoy the life you have, Cathy."

Cathy watched Grace trundle off to the High Street. Her own direction lay the other way, beyond the church grounds and over the road to the path by the bridge that led down to the tow-path. But Cathy lingered awhile. She hadn't quite finished her other conversation.

Chris was paying full attention to Sam's instructions and advice, only occasionally glancing at Dave for help.

"So the waste is stored in the tank under the bed, meaning you sleep over the poo. Mum says it's a passion-killer but that I'm too young to understand what she means."

"Indeed," said Chris.

"You're only taking her out for the afternoon so you won't need the night rules."

"No, Sam." *I have more than enough day rules to be getting on with, thanks.*

"The boat is six feet ten inches wide, so it's very narrow. You'll catch your side on the pull-down knob for the table and bash your head somewhere because you're tall. I don't bash my head or catch myself on things."

"Yes, well, I think I've…"

"Also, you'll pass boats called 'Living The Dream'. Do not laugh or mock them. We respect all canal users."

"Absolutely, Sam. Where would we be without respect?"

"Okay, Chris," said Dave. "She's all yours."

"He means the boat, not me," said Sam.

"Chris knows what I mean, and he doesn't want a little chatterbox like you aboard when he's trying to relax with Cathy."

"Cathy's a chatterbox too, isn't she?" said Sam.

Chris smiled. He could imagine Cathy at eight being just like Dave's daughter.

"I'll pass on your thoughts, Sam," he said. "She'll be along in a minute."

He looked up to the bridge over the canal, but it wasn't Cathy coming down the path.

Oh great…

Cathy eventually came down the path by the bridge and waved to Dave and Sam, who were down below on the tow-path going under the bridge. Ahead, she spotted Chris and Vic. They were occupying a bench just along from the Mary-Lou.

"I hope Dave hasn't left you in charge of his boat?" she called to Chris as she approached.

"He certainly has – and now I've been fully trained by Sam, I'll be taking you out for a cruise."

"Seriously?"

"Don't sweat – we won't be crossing the Atlantic."

"Right… well… great," said Cathy as she joined them. "You know Vic…?"

"Yes, of course. How are you, Vic?"

"Oh, I'm fine. I was just wondering about lunch. Chris said you might be bringing supplies?"

"Yes…" She shot a look at Chris, the useless twit.

"I thought we'd better have lunch on the tow-path," said Chris. "I don't want to make a mess on the Mary-Lou."

"Mess? I wasn't planning a chimp's tea party."

"Never mind all that," said Chris. "I verily bring news of great import regarding your foe, the accursed Lord Tyler."

"Have you been drinking the canal water?"

"Tyler's ancestor Jeremiah Dupris bought De Gaul Castle in 1677, Cath. From a man called Henry Lincoln."

"What are you talking about?"

"I just told you. Tyler's ancestor bought the castle…

for a pound."

"Now you're making things up."

"No, I'm serious. Look, I'll put my serious face on."

Chris spent the next few minutes talking Cathy through a photo he'd taken of the document he'd found.

"Right," said Cathy. "I'll text him the terrible news."

"No need. I've already told him. I didn't want you provoking him into drastic action."

"I see... so what did he say?"

"He said he'd be closing the castle with immediate effect."

"What? Oh Chris, you absolute—"

"Twit?"

"Yes, twit."

"Do you share Chris's passion for the waterways?" Vic asked.

Cathy took a moment to compose herself.

"Not as such, Vic. The canal always looks so peaceful though. I suppose we have the Victorians to thank for that."

For some reason, Chris was staring at her wide-eyed and making subliminal head-shaking movements.

"You're dead right, Cathy," said Vic, "but that's only half the story. While we have lunch, I'll explain all. Perhaps I should start at the beginning with Cressy."

"No!" cried Chris, who then rapidly adjusted his tone. "I mean no, I can tell Cathy all about Tom Rolt later."

"Alright," said Vic. "While we eat, I'll tell you both about Stourbridge. It's not for the faint-hearted, though. I'm talking about..." he looked left and right, like a desperado checking the coast was clear, "...direct action."

"Did you bring any beer?" Chris asked, looking somewhat deflated.

"It was 1961," said Vic, "and the Government had set

up a committee to consider the future of unviable canals. Anyway—"

"The direct action bit," said Cathy. "Tell me about that."

"Oh… well… by the early sixties, commercial traffic had ceased and the canal at Stourbridge was overgrown and in a bad way. In some parts it was so silted up, you could walk across. Certain persons decided to take direct action in breach of the law."

"Who?" said Chris, trying to show a bit of interest.

"They shall remain nameless, in case of legal action."

"It was over half a century ago," Chris pointed out. "I don't think…"

But Cathy shushed him and nodded to Vic.

"Go on, Vic."

"Right, so the British Waterways Commission said they would close the Stourbridge Canal and fill it with concrete – all done on the basis that it wasn't a navigable waterway. At first, the volunteers offered to dredge it to make it navigable, but British Waterways refused permission for any volunteer to enter the canal-side and they even threatened to get the police there to arrest trespassers. All was lost, Cathy – or so it seemed."

"It's like a movie," said Chris. "Bruce Willis could play Tom Rolt."

"Be quiet," said Cathy.

"Well," said Vic. "A hero rose from the ranks. David Hutchings."

He looked to Cathy and then Chris, then, clearly working out they had never heard of him, he continued.

"David Hutchings took direct action by breaking the law. He drove a powered drag line along the tow-path to scoop enough silt away to let a small boat through – just to prove the route to Stourbridge was still navigable, you see. He was threatened with prosecution, but, like Winston Churchill during the War, David did what had to be done, and said to hell with the consequences. I tell you, Cathy, Chris, I am humbled to report that David continued his illegal efforts and got a hundred boats through."

"Wow," said Cathy.

"David had taken on Goliath and won."

"That's um... that's really impressive," said Chris.

"Indeed so," said Vic. "There was a big party at the other end and the whole thing hit the front pages of the national newspapers. Well, blow me down if more and more people didn't flock to Stourbridge to see what all this canal rescue to-do was about. And, all the while, the evil pen-pushing Nazi force known as Government Officials could only look on with hate in their hearts and defeat in their eyes."

"And you were there, Vic?" asked Cathy.

"Yes, as a boy, I was there to salute a hero and cheer home those boats. It stoked my heart with a passion I have held onto ever since."

"I can see that," said Chris.

"Over the next few years, as a teenager, I got stuck into helping with the restoration of the sixteen locks at Stourbridge. And, as a young man, I was involved in the attempts to reopen the town arm to navigation in the seventies."

Cathy patted him on the arm. "Vic, this country owes you and those other fearless volunteers a great debt. Thank you."

"That's very kind of you to say so," said Vic prior to blowing his nose.

"Three cheers for Vic," said Cathy. "Hip-hip...

Chris looked at her as if she were mad – but joined her

in giving three hoorays.

Vic beamed. "Thanks Cathy. I rarely get that kind of response."

"Yes, thanks for all you've done," said Chris. "Cathy's right. You really are a marvel."

"Thank you," said Vic, looking like he might need to dab his eyes.

"So, breaking the law…" Cathy mused.

"What?" said Chris.

Vic opened a beer. "Yep, breaking the law. That was the key to it."

"Cathy, I hope you're not planning to overreact as usual," said Chris.

"Trespass," she uttered to no one in particular.

Chris was confused – and slightly annoyed.

"Vic, this is all your fault. Why can't you keep your trap shut?"

24

The Dream

After a canal-side lunch, Cathy and Chris boarded the Mary-Lou. Vic tried to board too, but Chris blocked him off.

"Sorry, Vic, Cathy and I have much to discuss, mano-a-mano... well, mano-a-wifo."

Chris fired up the engine and eased the boat away from the bank.

"Bye Vic," Cathy called. "Great talking with a man of passion."

Vic perked up and strode off with a spring in his step.

"Now there are some rules aboard the boat, Cath."

"As long as you know them, we'll be fine. I just want to enjoy the view."

"Yes, well, please note that the boat is very narrow inside. You'll catch yourself on the pull-down knob for the table, so watch out for that. Oh, and we might pass boats called 'Living The Dream'. Do not laugh or mock them."

"Or talk to them. Sounds like hours of boringly obvious guff before they break into a chorus of We Did It Our Way."

"Well, we're on the water now," said Chris, prior to taking a deep lungful of fresh air and still quite liking the name 'Living The Dream'. "Romantic, isn't it, Cath. The water, the scenery, the wind in our hair…"

"We're doing two miles an hour, Chris. There is no wind."

"It's a metaphorical wind."

"Well, okay, it's lovely."

Chris put his arm around Cathy and they stared ahead, with the metaphorical wind in their hair.

"Ah, the stress-free life," Chris sighed.

"Hey! Move over!"

Chris looked round to see a boat coming up behind them.

"What are you going so bloody slow for?" the boat's captain called over.

"Calm down," said Chris, "This is a stress-free environment."

"It will be when I get past you!"

"Let him go," said Cathy. "I don't want you tearing his tiller off and shoving up his nose. Not that he doesn't deserve it."

Chris steered the Mary-Lou closer to the bank, while the other boat – 'The Annual Bonus' – overtook.

Chris laughed and hugged Cathy. "Yes, this is the life."

"You and water, Chris. Are you sure you weren't born in a lake?"

"No, but…"

If he had a passion for anything outside of his relationship with Cathy, it was with the water. Could he make a livelihood out of that? Could he bring a sense of purpose to the way he made his money?

"I do see a possible future in a water-related business, Cath. What would you think of us running a bustling canal-side pub? Wouldn't it be a great way to live?"

Cathy pulled away from her man.

"If you recall, I overheard you talking about that."

"Ah yes, I forgot you're double-o-three and a half."

"So I looked into it."

"You did?"

"I'm sure you're aware that pubs are closing every day all over Britain. It's not a good business model anymore."

"We're talking about a waterside pub."

"It's still a pub."

"We could put a restaurant in."

"Restaurant failure rates are even worse than pubs. You'd just be pointing two Titanics at the same iceberg."

"I was thinking if we shared a passion for something… you know, put heart and soul into it…"

"Pubs and restaurants are the last place we want to put our heart and soul into. We can't afford to throw away everything we've worked for."

"I know, but I don't want to be Laptop Man. I've come to sense a gap in my life. Like there's something missing."

"Well…"

"And no, I don't mean children. I mean a driving force."

"And this has been festering since… all the time I've known you?"

"No, since you said my collectibles idea was rubbish. I was thinking how I've become a bit of a passenger, and, well…"

"You've never been a passenger, Chris."

"I was thinking I need to find a bit of passion for what

I do. It's obvious the only thing I love – apart from you – is coming down to the water. And so I've started thinking of a way to make that work for us. That's why I suggested Tyler should get involved. He's got money. He could make things happen."

Cathy shook her head. "Bad move."

"Killjoy."

"I'm a realist, Chris. But hear me out. I might not be skipping for joy down the tow-path, but that doesn't mean I didn't think about how to make it work."

"Go on then. I'm all ears – although I don't think you understand it like me. I've been among the canal folk."

"My view is that you, *yourself*, should look at ways to open a 50-berth marina with secure long-term and short-stay mooring, secure car parking, boat hire from a half-day to a month, and provide a kind of hub in the lost pub building. There you could have a bar, serve hot food, have a gym, showers, and a spares and provisions store. A beer garden would also be a winner in the summer. My research shows that the fun of cruising the canal system is diminished by the difficulty of finding overnight mooring that isn't within earshot of busy road traffic. Castle Hill's main roads are on the other side of town. Plus, most boat people won't be local. They'll travel a hundred miles to find a great marina."

"Yes, well, obviously you too understand the canal way of life."

"Thank you."

"No, actually, what you've just said… that absolutely nails it. Just one problem. Where do I get the big bucks to pay for it all?"

"I think you know where to go for the big bucks."

"You just said involving Tyler would be a bad move."

"Tyler owning everything would be a bad move. Tyler

investing in you would be different."

"Right. I see. It doesn't change the main problem. I'm still a long way from persuading him."

"You've only just got started, Chris."

"That's true."

"And once you get going… well…!"

Cathy returned to his embrace and Chris sighed contentedly. The view ahead was stunning. Maybe the canal really did offer them a future. And as for getting Shane Tyler to part with his cash? He would work on that another time. After all, you had to have the dream before you could live it.

25

Farewells...?

The following morning, while Cathy showered, Chris munched on toast in front of breakfast TV. As there was an election looming, it was necessary for the Prime Minister to be filmed in a classroom of small children while pretending to be interested in their ocean scene paintings.

Chris liked that. Not the PM being there, but the fact it took him back to his own early schooldays. All that painting and gluing stuff together. Such fun. Quite why any politician thought people looked at them more sympathetically because they were with kids... and it far was too early for school, meaning those poor mites had been dragged there by parents desperate to get junior's face on TV.

Soulless publicity stunts. He thought to mention it to Cathy when she came down – but then he recalled her own daft publicity stunt using kids. Mind you, that backfired when the main photo in the local paper was of

Cathy holding a terrified infant.

Kids in class though…

He had an idea. Why not point out to Cathy that all that PR stuff was fake, but there was nothing wrong with proposing a real, genuine classroom in the castle, where visiting schoolkids could enjoy a real history lesson.

Half an hour after Chris had randomly launched into something about having a castle classroom, and speckling her front with toast crumbs as he spoke, Cathy rang Kay's bell. Her focus was on something more urgent. Sometimes you know your time is up, but why go out with a whimper?

Kay welcomed Cathy into her home for coffee, but her smile had turned to a frown on hearing Cathy's words.

"Could you repeat that?"

"We're going ahead," said Cathy. "We'll break in and celebrate the July Festival this weekend."

"In April? Is that a good idea?"

"Chris thinks I'm insane, but I can't think of a better way to sign off. I made promises to people and to Castle Hill. I intend to keep my word."

"Even if it gets us into trouble?"

"I'll be able to sleep at night knowing I did the right thing."

"What about Shane Tyler?"

"He's an inflexible businessman. He'll be able to sleep whatever he does. Besides, he'll be in New York."

"Right…"

"I've told the Three Counties Re-enactment Society it's all systems go. Plus, we'll have a kids' mediaeval sports day, jousting, a barbecue, and fireworks. Obviously, we won't be able to advertise it to the public until Saturday, when Tyler's gone. I'm arranging to have instant posters appear in every shop window and flyers to every home in a three-hour publicity blitz."

"Are you and Chris in agreement on this?"

"Chris says I'm nuts. He did come up with a good idea though. A kids' history class – you know, stories, drawing…"

"I like it."

"Great, because I do need to push on with this. If I stop to think about it too long, I might agree with Chris that I've gone insane."

"And Chris is helping, is he?"

"A hundred percent."

Cathy felt good saying that. There would be no room for doubt once they got going.

An hour after breakfast, Chris was standing on the towpath, hands thrust deep into pockets, looking up and down the canal. There was no dream. There would be no narrow boat. No marina. No future in Castle Hill. He had texted Shane Tyler to say farewell. He didn't mention Tyler putting a couple of million into something that Cathy and Chris would control. In the harsh light of day, the idea seemed desperate.

No, they would return to London and get back to normal. Castle Hill would be a buoyant memory, but nothing more.

"Ahoy there!" It was Vic coming down from the bridge.

Chris smiled.

One last time.

"I won't be in Castle Hill much longer, Vic. We're

going back to London."

"Right."

"Not that I want to, but work calls."

"Well, you take care of yourself and that fine wife of yours. She'd have done a grand job back in the day fighting to save the canals."

"Maybe so. I've enjoyed our talks, Vic. I didn't appreciate these waterways enough, but you steered me straight. These canals are a national treasure and it's thanks to people like you we didn't lose something precious."

"It's a new era, Chris. A golden era. The working boats were coming to an end, but the canals are thriving now in a new way. We owe it all to people who knew when to do the right thing."

"You were one of them, Vic."

"I did a bit, I suppose. Did you know it took us three years to clear the entire Stourbridge Canal?"

"No, I didn't."

"Well, the authorities gave up in the end and came round to our way of thinking. We also had a bit of luck when Barbara Castle, the new transport minister, turned out to be a fan of the canals…"

Here we go…

"Are you alright, Chris?"

Chris smiled.

"I'm fine, Vic. You were saying?"

"Well, she brought in a Transport Act in 1968 that renamed many canals as cruise ways – set aside for tourism and leisure. We'd won, Chris. And that meant local groups looked to take on bigger and bigger restoration jobs, bringing even more canals back to life. Do you know there are now more narrow boats than there were in the 19th century? Two hundred thousand people spend their summer holiday on a canal boat. That makes the hairs stand up on my neck. To think we were told nobody wanted the canals, that they should all be closed and filled in. We fought and we won. My only regret is most of the heroes aren't known to us today."

"Surely everyone knows Tom and Angela Rolt."

"Yes, if it weren't for Tom and Angela on Cressy, and Tom writing that book, you wouldn't have all these wonderful canals full of people enjoying themselves. The irony being Tom wanted to save the canals for commercial use, not for fun. He'd have seen everyone on the canal and he would have yelled: bloody tourists!"

Chris laughed. "I can picture it."

"Always be vigilant, Chris. If you're passionate about something, always be prepared to fight for it. Remember, in the sixties, the Stourbridge Canal and its Town Arm had fallen into dereliction. It's now home to wonderful moorings. And the canal-side Bonded Warehouse there? In the eighties, the authorities wanted to demolish it. We fought the brainless twits, Chris. We fought them and won again. That building... it's now been restored and has won civic awards for its new role as a community facility. Never let faceless bureaucrats have the last word."

"Don't you worry, Vic. I'm a convert. I'll bend the ear of anyone who even so much as looks at the canal."

"So when are you leaving?"

"Oh, after the weekend. Monday, I suppose. I just need to hire a small van to load up our stuff. Today is a chance to say farewell to a few people."

"People like me, you mean."

"Yes, Vic.

Vic nodded. "So... Cathy's accepted her fate."

"Yes. She wants to do something at the castle tomorrow, but yes – she's accepted her fate. I texted

Shane Tyler. He's off to New York in the morning. I just wanted to tell him there were no hard feelings. He's doing his best and Cathy and I understand that."

"You'll be able to expand on that sentiment, Chris. Here he comes."

"Ah…"

"I'll be off down to Dean's mooring then," said Vic. He held out a hand. Chris shook it. "He's taking me for a ride to lunch – somewhere he knows where there's a waterside pub."

"Sounds fun, Vic. You take care, my friend."

Shane Tyler didn't look very relaxed for a man on the canal-side. Chris assumed victory would have set him at ease.

"Alright, Shane?"

"Yeah, just a million things going on. You know how it is."

"Er…"

"So you guys are leaving Castle Hill. I'll be sorry to see you go."

"I doubt that. We've both been a pain."

"Not at all. You both have passions. I get that."

"Everyone has passions, Shane."

"No, they don't. Not at all. Many people do jobs they have no love for and watch TV that distracts them from the reality of having no passions to fire them up, to wake them each morning, to drive them through the day, to make each evening a time to reflect on what they've achieved. These are the joys of the heart, Chris. You don't get them watching soaps."

"Tough words, Shane."

"I fought for what I wanted from life."

Chris sensed an opportunity.

"People can work too hard, Shane. Passions can

become obsessions." He tried to freeze out thoughts of Cathy. "Didn't you say that about your dad?"

"True. He was definitely an obsessive. He drove his business like a racing car. Top speed…"

"You're not like that."

"I'm trying to keep a part of me outside of the businesses I run. It's not easy. That's why I love to get out on the ocean. It's freedom, Chris. It's also bloody near impossible to find crew at the drop of a hat. I have to plan well in advance. Then my week on the yacht usually coincides with important meetings."

"So the yacht sits idle."

"Fully crewed and idle. Yes."

Chris could feel Shane's frustration. He could also feel the stress.

"So your dad was a workaholic, and now you're becoming one too – even though you know it's not good for you."

"When Dad died it was the biggest shock ever. And at the same time, I wasn't at all surprised. It's a strange one, Chris – shock and expectancy."

"Dads, eh?" said Chris. "Mine was the same. He had a hectic job, but was always selling stuff on the side for extra money. I say on the side – it took up as many hours as his main job. I always had a sense of him living at a hundred miles an hour. The best bit of luck I had was he loved to take time out fishing. Not often, maybe once a month, but occasionally I'd go with him. That's when I really got to know him."

"I never had that. I wish I had."

"Life's precious, Shane. It's a pity you don't have a floating relaxation base that's always ready for you."

"You mean have my own long boat?"

"Er, narrow boat. Long boats were the Vikings."

"Just kidding, Chris. No, I'm thinking you're wrong. I'm thinking I don't have time for narrow boats."

"That's your problem right there. You don't have time. When did we arrive at that point as a species?"

"It's too easy to say we should make time. The reality's different."

"Your dad's catchphrase?"

"Oww, low punch, mate."

"Sorry. I was just trying to say it can be done. I always make sure I make a little time for me."

"That's why you're broke, Chris."

"I'm not broke. A little short some months, perhaps – but I'm rich in spirit and last time I had a medical, I had low blood pressure."

"Don't talk to me about blood pressure. My doc is threatening to put me on tablets."

"You need to slow down. Not every day, not every week. But every now and again, you need somewhere you can be quiet and move slowly. It'll add years to your life."

"You're a tough man to argue with, Chris. I'm still not sure though. I'm bound to get some yacht-time at some point."

"You need an outlet where you can just turn up."

"I could book into a health spa for that."

"A health spa? When God's own canal is waiting here for you? Think of it. No hot pebbles on your back or incense candles. Just a beer and a view that changes at three miles an hour. It's exactly what you need. I'll be your beer partner if you want. I mean you can't have any corporate types on board. That would defeat the object."

"I don't know. It's a tempting prospect."

"Come on, Shane. How many health-improving scenarios involve beer and fishing?"

"Well…"

"Come on, you'll be based in Sydney, London, New York and Castle Hill. If you invest in me and my marina idea, we'd be partners."

"That's ballsy talk, Chris. I thought you wanted me to invest in the marina and you'd run a pub next door."

"I talked to Cathy."

"Now why am I not surprised?"

"I once set out to buy Cathy the perfect gift. Not easy. But I'm guessing if your dad were alive today, your perfect gift to him would be a narrow boat and a mooring at Chris and Cathy Chappell's brand new Castle Hill Marina."

Shane sighed and Chris hoped – even though he wasn't entirely sure where he and Cathy would be on Monday.

"Chris, I'll think about it."

26

Spies

Chris met Cathy at the bottom of the hill below the castle. For some reason, they were going to enter the old place like a couple of 12th Century spies. He wasn't too keen on any of it. Cathy was acting irrationally.

All the same, they headed up the hill. And then they veered off the path.

"Where are we going?" Chris asked.

"To anyone looking out from the keep, we're just two people having a walk around the castle. In no way could it be construed we're heading for the front door."

Chris shook his head.

"So what is the point of our unofficial visit?"

"To steal a set of keys."

"Keys to the castle?"

"Yes."

"You had a set. Why didn't you have copies made?"

"Because I didn't expect a big-headed show-off to turn up in a helicopter."

"So where do we get a set of keys?"

"I'm fairly certain Tyler put my keys in the office drawer desk."

"Right, so we break in, steal your keys and get out again."

"Guy de Gaul stood bravely on this hillside many a time, Chris. Try to channel a little of that. Besides, we don't have to break in. There's an architect up there, no doubt planning where to install the sauna and hot tubs."

They passed the ramp that went up to the main entrance and headed for a stroll around the perimeter – except, once they were past the point of being seen from a window, they doubled back and climbed up the steeper side of the ramp to reach the gate.

The gate itself was closed but not locked. A sign warned the public that De Gaul Castle was 'closed until further notice'.

Cathy pushed the left hand door open a crack and spied inside.

"All clear," she whispered.

They crept inside, where Cathy led them to the side of the porta-loos.

"Is that him?" said Chris. He'd spotted a man in a business suit by the rear tower. He was studying an iPad.

"Must be," said Cathy.

"So what do we do? Do we hide here until he's within arrow-shooting distance? Or do we go over and say hello?"

"We stay here until we can get the keys without being seen. I don't want Tyler knowing I was here."

"So the keys are in the office, which is across an open courtyard, which is visible from any point in the castle."

"He's bound to wander off to measure something. We'll be fine."

"Is this how it ends? With us arrested? With you being thrown out of British Heritage?"

"Don't exaggerate."

"Why don't we just go back to London and become one of those professional couples? I'll get an office job in IT somewhere."

"I think he's gone. Come on."

They set off but got just a few yards before Chris realized the architect was just inside the rear tower doorway.

"Back, back," he gasped.

"Quick, in there," said Cathy.

Chris followed her into the ladies' porta-loo, which he feared had added to the list of charges heading his way.

"Oh crap, he's coming," said Cathy, peering through the crack in the ajar door.

"It's like Napoleon," said Chris. "We've met our Waterloo. Or, in this case, our porta-loo."

"Shut up, Chris."

Chris peered out through the crack alongside his wife. Fortunately, the architect walked past to enter the men's porta-loo.

"Come on," said Cathy. "We need to be fast."

They hurried out of the loo, across the courtyard and into the office, where Cathy checked the drawer.

"They're not here. Have a look around."

Chris glanced at the desk... and the plans laid out on it. One sheet had a design for a plaque featuring a black raven.

"You seen this, Cath?"

"Keys, Chris. Keys."

They found them by the printer.

"Let's go," said Cathy.

"Too late," said Chris. "He's coming into the office."

"Quick, in there."

They hurried into the recently rediscovered adjoining room. To Cathy, moving the bookcase to find a hidden door seemed to have happened in a previous lifetime.

"Just be quiet until he's gone," she advised.

Chris's phone rang – quite loudly.

"Haven't you heard of silent mode, you nitwit?"

Chris answered it as they stepped out of the room, pretending they hadn't seen the architect standing over the drawings on the desk.

"Chris, you've talked me into it," said Shane Tyler on the other end of the line. "Let's sort something out. I want you in up to your neck on this though. Don't leave it with me or it won't happen."

"I'll drink to that, Shane," said Chris. "At least I will once we reopen the lost pub."

He thought it best not to mention that he and Cathy had broken into the castle. He didn't want to spoil the mood.

As they made their way across the courtyard, Cathy nudged her husband,

"Does that mean Tyler's interested?"

"Yes. But I'm thinking we should have a big stake in it. I'm thinking we could sell our place in Finchley, pay off the mortgage, and invest in the marina. You know, have a proper stake in it so we can be taken seriously."

"It's a big step. I'm not sure."

"I'm also thinking about this festival thing tomorrow. Is it such a good idea?"

"What?"

"I'm just wondering if it might be better to cancel it. We don't really want to upset Shane, do we?"

"Christopher Chappell?"

"Yes?"

"Consider yourself banished from this castle."

Chris stepped outside. A moment later, Cathy came out to join him.

"Sorry," she said. "I didn't mean that."

"That's okay. I think Shane might be about to back my marina plan. I don't want to jeopardize it."

"I understand."

"You're not going to cancel tomorrow, are you?"

"Stop worrying. Tyler's going to be thousands of miles away in New York."

"True…"

They started down the hill, looking out over the town… in much the same manner as Hugh de Gaul observed those gathering against him at a time his brother Guy seemed incapable of holding on to his courage. Strong hearts were needed…

"When did I start to turn into a sour person?" Cathy asked.

"What? You haven't. And you never will."

"Something's changing in me, Chris. I wasn't always like this. I used to share my positive side with everyone – whether they wanted it or not. Now I limit it to little bursts when I'm in the mood. And I'm not in the mood as much as I used to be."

"Things take their toll, Cath. Moving here was a big step."

"Is it possible for someone's soul to start drying out?"

"Only if they leave it out in the sun too long."

Cathy stopped.

"I don't want to be that person, Chris."

Chris stopped and turned to face her.

"I know."

"I don't want to dispense fewer and fewer minutes of kindness each day. I want to be me again."

"You've always been you."

"Have I?"

Chris looked into her eyes.

"You've had to put up with a lot, but we can agree we're over it now. We can start a new future where we concentrate on us."

Cathy nodded.

I can see inside that head of yours. You're wondering if you can grit your teeth and embrace those friends who are new mums. And what of your sister's bump? Could you give that the royal treatment? Would no detail of its progress be too small to enjoy?

"I just have to get through tomorrow, Chris. I want to have a big successful day where I sign off with a bang. Will you support me?"

"I don't know, Cath. I think it's time we switched to Team Tyler."

"Well, just so you know, I'm seeing Kay to plan things. I'll be in late. And I'll be going out early. If we don't get a chance to talk, at least wish me luck."

"I've always wished you that, Cath."

At the bottom of the hill, Cathy turned right for Castle Close. Chris let her go and headed the other way. Beyond the High Street and the church, he rejected the path down to the canal, choosing instead to follow the road that led out of town but, he knew, offered a turn off that passed by the lost pub.

Five minutes later, standing in the beer garden, he tried to picture it – the pub reborn as the marina HQ, with the bar and restaurant full of happy customers, with the marina full of boats, with sunlight glinting off the water...

"I'd normally say it's your decision, Cath," he said to the water. "But I can't do that this time."

Cathy nodded, he imagined.

"Of course you can't this time," he felt she would say.

"You turned into a mind reader, have you?"

"You can't leave this one to me because it's your passion."

"That's a funny word to use."

"Yes, Chris, the man who isn't much bothered about anything has found a dream."

"I don't like that word either. One minute we're happy in London, the next you're having a dream and getting passionate about a castle."

"I'm glad you've found a passion for something. I'd like to share it. If you're in the mood to share...?"

"Cathy, I dread what business nonsense I'm about to come up against. I won't do it without you. I want us to be passionate together. What do you say?"

What would Cathy say for real?

He thought they could give the lost pub a proper name. The Castle. She would like that. She told everyone she was coming to Leicestershire to run a castle, and now she would. She'd give him the biggest, tightest hug too.

"No, we should call it the Narrow Boat Inn," she would say. "We don't want to confuse people."

The Narrow Boat Inn...

With Cathy on board, it would be a friendly, family place with hot meals served all day and an outdoor play area for children. Life in Castle Hill, he felt, had the potential to be brilliant.

27

Into Battle

Outside the castle gate, Cathy looked down on the inspiring sight of the Three Counties Re-Enactment Society's 'Stephen versus Matilda' battle. The way the clashing forces engaged thrilled her…

…and shook Hugh de Gaul to the core. He was fighting against all odds to save, if not the lives, at least the honor of those who supported the primrose emblem. They had to hold on. They had to!

Ever since her first visit to Castle Hill with dopey boyfriend Garth, Cathy had looked forward to returning to enjoy another big festival, with the entire hill transported back to the 12th Century. Now it was happening – with her at the helm.

What fun!

She had promised the town it would be the best festival yet and it seemed to be the case so far. She was adamant that no bored, rich twit was going to pull the plug and make her look stupid.

"Where's Chris?" asked Grace, appearing at Cathy's side. "Not down the pub, is he?"

"I don't know," said Cathy – which was true. For the first time in their relationship, they hadn't spoken to each other beyond a goodnight and good morning. It wasn't something she wished to experience again, but Chris had made headway with Shane Tyler, so – maybe they were down the pub together. Although wasn't Tyler due to fly off to New York?

"It's a wonderful spectacle, Cathy," said her predecessor, Henry. "You know I doubted you were the right person for the job, but I was wrong. You're exactly what De Gaul needs to carry the sword."

"Thanks Henry. I'm not sure Mr Tyler would agree with you."

They went inside, where people were beginning to gather in readiness to sample Dean's offerings at the barbecue.

Cathy began to wonder where she was headed in life. This is what she wanted. And now Chris wanted something different. That was good though. She was glad he'd developed a passion for something. It had long been clear to her that he had a lot to offer, should he ever find something he could believe in. But now life seemed intent on pulling them in two directions.

Just then, a sword-wielding Norman knight came through the gate – although this one was wearing jeans and a rugby shirt.

"Hello love. I thought I'd come and defend the castle from Australian marauders."

"You daft big twit."

"This broadsword's heavy though. If I swing round like this I… arghh."

The weight of the enormous sword continued Chris's

momentum, sending him through a stack of cardboard boxes containing the soft toys that would be children's prizes later.

"Put that thing down before you decapitate half a dozen Tiggers!" Cathy demanded.

Chris steadied himself and handed the sword back to the plumber-cum-knight he'd borrowed it from.

Then Cathy gave him a hug.

"I love you, you big oaf."

"I love you too, you nutcase."

"Let's make this the best day ever, then we'll work out what to do next."

"Agreed."

"Cathy?" It was Kay by the gate. "Liz is coming up the hill."

"Ah great."

Cathy explained to Chris that canal regular Liz had volunteered to help maintain order at the top of the keep – which, with lots of kids around, Cathy wouldn't open to the public until she had a couple of people in place.

"I'll catch up with you later," Cathy said as she departed to greet Liz.

"Chris?" It was canal volunteer Dean calling from the barbecue. "You couldn't take over for a couple of minutes, could you?"

Chris assumed command of the burgers while Dean popped to the porta-loo. It was clear Cathy had organized everything really well. There were lots of smiling faces and plenty of activities going on. There would even be fireworks later.

Then he spotted a familiar face entering the courtyard.

"Jasmine! Fancy a burger?"

"Um, no, I've just had an organic guacamole salad, thanks. Is Cathy about?"

"She's probably at the top of the keep. Can I help?"

"Those records you found...?"

"Not more bad news for Shane Tyler?"

"No, this relates to Cathy."

"Please tell me you've found something that links her to the castle."

"I have."

"You have? Brilliant!"

"Not brilliant, Chris, but historically important."

"Right, go on..."

"One of Cathy's ancestors did build part of the castle."

"Oh Jasmine, that's all she's ever wanted."

"Frederick Barrett."

"Wow... no, hang on, wasn't he Cathy's sawmill guy?"

"Yes, he also worked as a builder for a time."

"Right, so... how did he build a Norman castle in the Victorian era? Time travel?"

"He didn't build the castle, Chris. He built that bit over there."

Chris followed her finger to the Victorian structure.

"You mean...?"

"Yes, Cathy's office."

Chris was aghast. "The one part of the castle she utterly despises... was the bit built by her family?" He stifled a robust urge to laugh. "Oh, what a surprise she's going to have. Or shock. Actually, it might be worth having an ambulance on standby."

"You think she might need medical assistance?"

"No, but whoever gives her the bad news might."

Chris spotted Cathy emerging from the keep and waved her over.

"Jasmine has news."

"It's about your family's connection to the castle."

"Oh?"

Jasmine explained which part of De Gaul Castle Frederick Barrett was responsible for. Cathy took a moment to absorb the information, although the look on her face suggested to Chris it was an inner journey from horror to disgust, with perhaps a short stop at disappointment along the way.

"You mean that heap of derelict rot we call an office... that's what my ancestor built?"

"You said you felt some kind of spiritual connection," said Chris. "As site manager, if you spot Frederick Barrett's ghost, you could ask him for a refund."

"A bodge-it builder," said Cathy. "I can't believe it."

"So... it looks like no-one can trace their family all the way back," said Chris.

"It's still important social history," said Jasmine. "Frederick didn't work as a builder or sawmill hand all his life. He ran a pub for a few years."

"How do we know that?"

"There are some details about his background in a court report in the local paper. He was caught watering down the spirits."

"What pub was it?" Cathy asked.

"The Queen's Arms in Field Way."

She showed them on a map. It was the lost pub.

"Incredible," said Chris.

"Right, this actually rings a bell," said Cathy. "When I was researching Frederick... yes, his parents Alfred and Eliza Barrett were running the Queen's Arms in 1851. They must have known the landlord when Frederick took a turn. They probably put in a good word for him."

"Frederick spent six months in prison," said Jasmine.

"I wonder if he bumped into any of his family?" said

Chris.

"That's not funny," said Cathy.

"Oh come on, we've had Ollie the Outlaw, now we've got Freddie the Felon."

Jasmine checked the notes on her iPad.

"Frederick's son Harry was born in 1876. And his grandson, Arthur in 1896. There's a sad bit – Arthur volunteered to fight in the First World War. He died during the Battle of the Somme in 1916."

An attention-grabbing noise cut through the moment. It was coming from above them.

"A helicopter!" exclaimed a small boy.

"It can't be him," said Chris. "He's on his way to America."

"It is him," said Cathy. "He's just sent me a text."

"What does it say?"

"It's only six words but I can't say five of them while there are children around."

"Well, he can't land here," said Chris. "The car park and road are too busy."

With Dean coming back from the porta-loo, Chris left his station, handed back the burger flipper and followed Cathy to the entrance. From there, they watched Tyler's helicopter land in the farthest part of the parkland.

"Ah, the wonderful few minutes of calm before the storm," said Chris.

They spent it waiting in silence, all the while watching the castle owner's progress from the aircraft, across the children's play area, past the public toilets, through the gap in the fence, and up the hill.

"What the hell is going on?" Shane Tyler finally got to say.

"I thought you were airport bound?" said Chris.

"Yes, by helicopter. I asked the pilot to fly over so I

could take one last look at my castle before I fly to New York. And what do I see? A bloody warzone!"

"Shall we go into the office?" Cathy suggested. "You don't want to look like the Grinch in front of children."

Shane Tyler barged past them.

A moment later, Cathy closed the office door for privacy. Tyler was first to speak.

"Well, before we get down to what action I might take, you may as well hear the good news. I've proved my family built the castle."

"Pardon me?" said Cathy.

"I've always felt it in my bones," said Tyler. "Now I have a written monograph from an Oxford historian."

"How much did you pay him?" said Chris.

"I've proven my connection to the original owners of this castle. The Courtenay family."

"That's not right," said Cathy.

"The De Gauls never owned the castle. It was always Courtenay Castle. The raven banner flew here. Not the primrose."

"This is all made up nonsense," said Cathy.

"He has a plan to rename it," said Chris. "I realize now I've seen the designs. That architect…"

But Tyler continued over him. "The Courtenays were Catholics so they lost the estate during the Reformation – that's Henry the Eighth to you. That's when your beloved de Gauls got the castle. My family simply bought it back when they were able to – hence that confirmation you found in those old muniments."

Chris shook his head. "This isn't right, Shane."

"You're a nice guy, Chris, but you know nothing about history."

"Cathy, I'm a hundred percent with you. Mr Tyler can do what he likes about the marina."

Cathy let out a short, sharp breath.

"British Heritage won't let you rename the castle."

"That's why he was doubly determined to close it for a year," said Chris. "So he could rebrand the place. What size are those raven plaques, Shane? Ten feet tall in polished chrome, so you can bolt them to all the walls? And all done without any nosy historians like Cathy or Kay around?"

"I think we're done," said Tyler. "I'll just call the police and have this invasion brought to a halt…"

Tyler got his phone out.

"Right…" said Cathy.

Fearing she might go outside and give an Agincourt speech to the re-enactment society, Chris took hold of Tyler's wrist, squeezed, and removed the phone from his weakened grip.

"Sorry, Shane, but I can't have you telling the police you're under siege at De Gaul Castle. Not while my wife's having one of her moments."

Chris accepted that any partnership with Shane Tyler was less likely now than Guy de Gaul turning up and reclaiming his property. He'd wanted to show Cathy he was a man who could launch a business based on his passion for the waterways.

Maybe he'd get a chance to say so during the court case.

28

Well, I Never!

Wary of an accusation of theft, Chris placed the confiscated phone in the desk drawer.

"I'm not staying here," said Tyler. "I'll go down to the police station."

"Sorry, Shane, but I can't allow that. I know I'm going to regret this, but no-one is stopping Cathy today."

Chris took a key he recognized from the drawer and invited Tyler to step into the room that had been discovered when Cathy decided to move the bookcase.

"What's this, a prison cell?" Tyler protested.

"I'm sure you'll get a great day in court over this."

"You cannot be serious. Cathy's in the wrong and you're helping her."

"That's how we roll, Shane. You wouldn't understand."

"Come on, buddy. We practically have a deal in place. That marina idea? I had my people check it out. The pub land is owned by some old guy with no means to do anything with it. I reckon we could get it for a knock-down price."

Chris closed the door on Shane Tyler and plonked himself down in Cathy's chair. There was no way he could allow any escape attempt. He supposed it wasn't the best way to build a relationship with the wealthiest man he'd ever met, but life seemed set on keeping Christopher Chappell in his place.

"I can't see a thing in here!" Tyler complained.

Chris sighed and got up. He grabbed the office torch from the desk drawer, opened the cell door, handed it over, and closed the door.

Having resumed his seat, Chris thought it still might be a good idea to be friendly to Shane. There was a billionth of a percentage chance they might one day laugh about this over a beer.

"Don't give up on Cathy," he advised. "She's special. Nuts, but special."

He thought of his own idea regarding a classroom. Cathy could have that one.

"I'm serious, Shane. You take the glass and steel construction you're planning once the office and junk sanctuary goes. Cathy reckons the building could stretch the full length of the courtyard. That way, you could include a classroom for kids. Imagine that. Schools could bring children up for a history lesson in a real castle. If that doesn't fire up their imaginations, nothing will."

He listened for a reply. There wasn't one.

"You would create a legacy, Shane. You hear me?"

Still there was no response.

Chris gripped the edge of his seat.

Oh God, not a cell suicide.

"Shane?"

He got up and listened.

There was a ghostly clanking sound.

Chris's eyes opened their widest since watching The Texas Chainsaw Massacre.

If he's done himself in, he's haunting the place pretty quickly.

The sound though... it wasn't coming from the cell. It was coming from below.

He bent down, close to the floorboards.

Clang.

He leapt up again, unlocked the door and...

The cell was empty.

Had the spooks taken him?

Chris turned his phone-torch on.

No, the old carpet had been rolled back. There was a trapdoor.

Chris lifted it. He could see the torchlight flashing around below. It seemed to be some sort of basement or cellar.

"Are you okay, Shane?"

"There's no way out," said Tyler.

Chris poked his head down the hole.

"Wow, a wine cellar."

"There's no wine," Tyler informed him. "Just weapons."

"Ah, that weird bloke they had here years ago. The Cold War guy."

Chris adjusted his position and lowered himself down.

"No need to come down, Chris. It's rotten and spooky. I'll sit quietly in the office. Cathy can have her moment. Come on, let's go."

Chris shrugged and half-heartedly flashed his own light across the space. He almost turned away but something...

"After you," said Tyler. "I'll give you a push then you can pull me up."

But Chris wasn't going anywhere.

"Come on," said Tyler. "We can talk about Cathy's idea. We'll fill the cellar in and put a fantastic structure on top... Chris?"

Even though it was partly obscured by a big empty wine rack, Chris had seen that emblem before.

On a gravestone.

On a ceiling.

And now it was carved into a mediaeval stone wall.

29

Now What?

Henry seemed to be in the way. Over the past few days, he'd been doing that a lot. Cathy didn't mind though. He had been in charge at De Gaul for thirty-two years and then a woman turns up from London and it's suddenly open season on hidden secrets coming to light.

She watched the last of the office floor being taken out by the team of archeologists, engineers and surveyors. Then someone began drilling with a long, thin diamond-tipped bit designed to put a small hole through the wall bearing the primrose symbol.

It was a pity Shane Tyler had pulled out, she felt. His money would be difficult to replace. It annoyed her that he could cause so much disruption before the final contracts were signed, and then be allowed to walk away as if nothing had happened.

A few noisy minutes later, the drilling stopped and a thumbs-up was given.

Next a tiny infra-red camera on the end of a pole was

pushed through.

Cathy stepped away to join Kay and Chris with the team monitoring events from a laptop inside the cleared-out storage area. Henry quickly joined them viewing the monochrome images.

"It seems to be snowing," he observed.

"Must be the dust," said Kay.

"It's clearing," said Cathy.

There were now around a dozen people trying to get a look.

"What's that?" Chris wondered.

The scene settled, the camera focused, and it appeared to be a chamber with bunks, three high, all the way down the right-hand side. Someone pushed the pole in a little further. Then the laptop woman toggled a joystick to turn the camera.

"Good God..." said Henry.

"Knights..." said Kay.

"Okay," a voice called. It sounded like the senior surveyor. "We'll remove a few blocks so we can get someone inside."

Cathy, Chris, Kay and Henry went out into the courtyard and took mugs of hot tea from the guy sorting out the food and beverages. Nobody spoke. It seemed too momentous for any pre-emptive views.

A long, tortuous half hour passed as a couple of blocks, low on the right, were very carefully removed and the hole braced.

"We're back," somebody called from the storage area.

Cathy and her team gathered again by the laptop. Someone was going in with a camera. It seemed to be Laura, the smallest of the archeologists. There was dust again. But it settled.

The camera moved in slowly. And turned. The nearest

bunk on the right contained a stone effigy of a reclining knight atop a casket. There was something engraved into the side. From the laptop, Cathy squinted to make it out.

"Benouet de Gaul."

She almost squealed.

The camera went in further. More bunks. More knights atop their caskets.

Frederis de Gaul.

Adam de Gaul. This one had the primrose emblem.

"There's the family line," said Kay. "Through the eldest son. Adam must go directly back to Guy de Gaul. We'll soon meet our hero."

"He'll be the last of them, by the castle's foundations," said Henry. "Oh, to meet the founder."

The camera continued its journey.

"It goes all the way under the keep!" said a voice from somewhere.

More caskets were studied.

Nicolas de Gaul.

Gabriel de Gaul. With a primrose.

The journey took in twenty more knights before it reached a final two. One low against the wall. One above it.

The camera homed in on the lower casket.

Guy de Gaul.

"The founder," someone uttered.

Cathy gasped. "No primrose."

The camera rose to the knight resting above Guy.

"Hugh de Gaul," said Kay.

"With a primrose unlike any of the others," said Henry.

"With leaves and a stem," said Cathy. "The source of all these other primroses."

"I think we might need to re-write the history books,"

said Kay.

"I think someone should tell Grace," said Chris.

Cathy stepped away.

"What a pity Shane Tyler couldn't be here to tell her," she said.

"Three million is a lot of money to lose," said Henry. "What a spot of luck we'll double that when this discovery puts us back on the map."

"The sponsorship offers will flood in," said Kay.

Cathy shook her head in disbelief. "We could stick with Mr Tyler's glass and steel bit, but go with Chris's idea to extend and include a classroom."

Kay nodded. "We could also have interactive displays at key points around the castle… like giant iPads on the wall. You press the screen icon to get video, photos, illustrations…"

"You'll face a lot of challenges," said Henry. "Visitor numbers will rise significantly."

Cathy agreed. "We'll need more staff, that's for sure. Kay, would you consider being the permanent, all-year-round, assistant manager?"

Later, out by the entrance, Cathy and Chris stood side-by-side, looking out over the town. Well, Cathy's eyes might have been on the town. Chris's gaze was to the river and the canal.

"You've got a bright future in Castle Hill," he said. "I can't tell you how glad I am it's all worked out."

"I'm sorry the marina didn't come to anything, Chris. I can see it… fifty narrow boats moored…"

"What's this? Marina talk?" It was Henry sneaking up on them. "Not that old chestnut."

"How do you mean?" said Chris.

"A friend of mine has been trying for years to get one put in near the church. No luck."

"The church?" said Chris. "Not by the lost pub?"

"What lost pub?" said Henry.

An hour later, Chris was meeting with Henry's friend, a Chamber of Commerce member in his sixties called Charles Grout, and explaining how the lost pub was the best site. Cathy was alongside him, ready to chip in.

It didn't take her long.

"In fact," she said, "we're selling our property in London to raise the money to kick-start it."

Chris gave her an 'are we?' look, but she simply smiled back at him.

"This sounds very exciting," said Charles. "I can't get down there on account of my legs. Motorcycle accident in my twenties, you know. I do love boats, though. I've said all along I'd put up a decent stake. You could be the missing piece, Chris."

"What, my money?"

"No, your passion. That's what's been missing. A man like you, full of passion for the project, is just what we need. I can think of two or three others who would be very interested in such a project."

"I don't know what to say," said Chris.

"Yes, he does," said Cathy. "He says what are we waiting for?"

30

A Place in the World

Two months later

The banqueting hall had never looked better in Cathy's time at De Gaul Castle. Henry said it hadn't looked better in his, either. The long primrose banner adorning one wall made a bold statement concerning the castle's heritage. The vases of flowers, including primroses, and the tables laden with cold buffet food made the hall feel welcoming. The warmth of early June only added to it.

At the far end of the hall the main attraction took pride of place.

An oil painting of Grace Darling.

It was something her father had paid for when she turned twenty-one, many years before. Recovered from her loft, it now stood, freshly framed, on a display easel. The card below described: 'Grace Hilda Primrose Darling, direct heir of Hugh de Gaul, founder of this castle'.

Cathy looked around at the guests dressed in their finest, as befitted the occasion. The evening's most important person, Grace, would be arriving soon with Kay.

Chris would be arriving soon too, although not in any planned way. She couldn't believe what the big oaf had done. She had been down in London for a week to see friends and, of course, her sister Jo, Boris the bump and Jo's boyfriend, Toby. No sooner she was on the train coming back, Chris texted her to say he'd be spending a few days with Dave on the Mary-Lou. They were taking a leisurely cruise to a) enjoy life, and b) check out some marinas for ideas.

She arrived home with three days to prepare for the big event at the castle while faced with Chris's vague promise he'd be back in time. A few choice words over the phone later and Chris was *guaranteeing* he'd be there for Saturday evening.

Cathy went outside and peered down the hill. There was no sign of him, so she ventured into the courtyard. As always these days, she was drawn to the site of her old office – no longer there and now replaced by a temporary structure with stairs down to the primrose wall. She decided not to descend the stairs – mainly because there were lots of tools and equipment to trip over. It would be impressive once it was finished, with a staff only staircase leading to a door for access, and a public staircase leading to an observation window beside the engraved primrose, enabling visitors to see the knights. Of course, in time, Tyler's glass and steel structure would house the whole thing, including two offices and, as per Chris's suggestion, a classroom. Cathy couldn't wait for it all to come to fruition. For now though, the extra porta-cabin in the courtyard that housed her office would have to suffice.

She returned to the entrance for another look.

And there he was – Lord Christopher of the Canal, hurrying up the hill... in a flippin' rugby shirt and jeans.

"Hello, love. I got here as soon as four-miles-an-hour would allow."

"Chris..."

"Hello," said Henry, appearing at Cathy's side, "looks like we're being invaded."

"Let's grab a drink, shall we?" said Chris, kissing Cathy and patting Henry's shoulder before going through into the hall.

Immediately, he took in the fifty or sixty invited guests who were there to celebrate the recent turn of events, checking their attire against his own. He guessed they smelled better than him too. Taking the philosophical view, he shrugged, grabbed a beer and joined Jasmine and Roland.

"If Cathy comes this way, just form a human wall in front of me. I think I've got a lecture coming."

"I think she just wanted you to be here," said Jasmine.

"And you are," said Roland, possibly eyeing Chris's trainers with a little too much of a frown.

Chris let Jasmine's ensuing conversation regarding travel wash over him. He smiled politely while mulling over options and actions regarding Castle Hill Marina.

A few minutes later, Kay, Cathy and Henry led Grace Darling in to a round of applause. She waved regally and then joined Chris, Jasmine and Roland.

"Hello Grace," said Chris. "You know what you need...?"

No sooner he'd said it, a waiter carrying a tray of filled champagne flutes arrived.

"Ooh, champagne," said Grace. "I don't normally drink champagne."

"No problem," said Henry, joining them, "I'll drink it for you."

"Hands off!" said Grace. "I meant I didn't drink champagne when I was a peasant. Now I'm practically Queen of England, I'll allow myself a glass or three."

Vic came over, looking resplendent in a navy blue blazer and crimson tie. Chris smiled. Well, Cathy had said he could invite a guest, and he chose Vic. Now he'd have to put up with it.

Vic was proffering a carrier bag.

"This is for you, Chris. A little token of friendship."

"Oh?"

Chris opened the bag and extracted an old book. He read the title.

"Narrow Boat by Tom Rolt. Ohhh Vic…"

"It's a signed first edition," said Vic. "Probably worth millions. Well, perhaps a hundred. It ought to be worth millions though. I mean when you think back to 1939…"

"Vic, this is an amazing gesture. I absolutely love it. Thank you a million times."

"I wanted you to have it. I mean I haven't got any family."

"Oh, I…"

"At least not any family who are interested in canals."

"Ah."

"You look after it, Chris."

"Best gift ever. I'll look after it same as you have."

"Good lad. Maybe you can share the stories about the early days. You know, spread the word, sort of thing."

Chris imagined himself pouring someone a drink at the bar of the marina HQ while explaining how Tom and Angela Rolt coming along in Cressy would have been the beginning of something special. Then he worried he might scare away all the customers.

"I'll tell you what I'll do, Vic. You and me are going to sit down and design a commemorative plaque. Then when the lost pub reopens as the marina HQ, we're going to put it on the wall in the bar area for generations of visitors to read."

"We'll never get everything on a plaque, Chris."

"No, it'll say something like… 'When you raise your glass here, the toast is always: To Cressy!' Then when the inevitable question comes over the bar, we can sell them a short booklet written by you. We'll charge 99p and the money can top up your pension."

"Well," said Vic. "I don't know what to say. I'm speechless."

Chris clinked his beer bottle against Vic's champagne glass.

"To Cressy!"

"To Cressy!" Vic echoed. "And all who sailed in her, bless 'em!"

Cathy let them sip their drinks and then leaned in close to Chris to whisper in his ear.

"I'd like a word with you, Christopher."

"Ah."

"Excuse us a minute, Vic," she said, prior to luring Chris away to a quiet corner.

"Everything alright, Cath? I don't smell that bad, do I?"

"I want you to steady yourself."

"Okay…"

"Ready?"

"Yes, how much trouble am I in?"

"I'm pregnant."

"Wow, *that* much trouble. Seriously, though…"

"I was too scared to say anything."

"What? Are you saying…?"

"I wasn't going to tell you on the phone or in a bloody text."

"Oh Cathy…"

"I just kept expecting it to be a false alarm. I know it's crazy. I mean I must have taken ten home pregnancy tests. Anyway, while I was having a great time with Jo and Boris the Bump, I slipped away for tests to make sure everything was okay. The anti-natal clinic did all the checks and said everything is absolutely fine. I'm ten weeks, Chris. No, *we're* ten weeks."

Chris felt his eyes pricking.

"I… well… yes…"

He stepped away, gathered himself, and raised his voice to full volume.

"Everyone outside, please. In front of the keep. Please don't argue."

He climbed the stairs, two at a time, to the top of the keep and was soon facing those gathering below.

"Citizens of Castle Hill," he bellowed. "I have news. Not news of taxes or war, but of a matter far more important. Christopher Chappell is going to be a dad! Yes! Yes! Bloody yes!"

Chris came hurrying down to share in the hearty congratulations already being offered to Cathy outside the gate.

"Bloody hell, Cath, that felt good."

As everyone made their way back inside, their arms wrapped around each other.

And the tears flowed.

"I love you, you big oaf."

"I love you too, you nutcase."

They pulled apart and beheld each other in a new light.

"Well…" said Cathy, sniffling.

"Yes, well…"

"Of course, tonight isn't about us."

"You're right. Go do your castle duties, mother-to-be."

"There's one thing I can do right away," said Cathy, dabbing her eyes.

She went off and grabbed Henry.

"I don't want you to argue with me, Henry. I want you to return to work at the castle on an 'hours that please you' basis. You retired too early and I don't want you to miss out on our glory years."

Henry looked shaken. "I don't know what to say, Cathy. It's... yes. Yes, please. And thank you. Chris was right about you. You really are..."

"Special?"

"Unpredictable."

Chris took a sip of his beer, looked out over Castle Hill, and let out a satisfied sigh. He could see now, more than ever, how history was all around them, still weaving its way through the fabric of every single life. Had there been no drunken party in Barfleur in 1120, the White Ship wouldn't have sunk, Henry I's heir William would have lived, and there would have been no fight between Stephen and Matilda or their on-off supporters and therefore no need for De Gaul castle, and no reason for Cathy to visit it as a girl who believed she had a connection to it, and who, as a direct result, developed a love of history and got a job with British Heritage, where she worked on events and met a young man called Chris.

Equally, had there been no Tom Rolt going on a trip aboard Cressy with his wife Angela in 1939, and writing up their adventures in his book Narrow Boat, there would very likely be no canals and therefore no group of volunteers for Chris to join, and no prospect of restoring the lost pub, and no future as a stakeholder in a thriving marina.

Cathy let Henry go back inside. It was funny how it had all fallen into place. How part of the castle's curtain wall tumbling down had taken a small tower with it and uncovered part of the tomb. How Jeremiah Dupris, who had only bought the castle a few years earlier with a desire to prove his raven symbol-bearing forbears had built the place, re-hid it beneath a new wooden building. And how her own ancestor had upgraded that building in Victorian times.

She turned to see Chris, facing away from her to the open view. Impossibly, at least for her, he was becoming an even better man. He had long been the partner she needed, but he was growing now, expanding his horizons. His confidence was increasing. His energy levels had been boosted. He whistled and sang even more. His zest for life was brimful. He had ideas. He was a real man of passion.

They each had their own thing now. Billy the Bump would grow up with passionate parents. One running an amazing castle, the other running a brilliant marina. They would never have a dull moment, immersed in their passions, sharing all their news, attempting to create more offspring, and having the time of their lives in Castle Hill.

She arrived at Chris's side. He said nothing, but his arm wrapped around her shoulders. Beyond the town, the river and the canal, the horizon was clear, giving Cathy hope that tomorrow would be a fine day. Then Chris gave her a squeeze and she knew that many, many more tomorrows would be fine too.

The End

Thank you for reading 'Cathy & Chris Under Siege' — I really hope you enjoyed it.

I don't have a giant publishing house working on my behalf so I'm reliant on good people like yourself helping me spread the word about my books. If you enjoyed reading this one and have a few minutes to spare, I would be eternally grateful if you could leave a review on Amazon. For feel-good fiction authors like me, it's the only way we can gain traction for our books (which allows us to write more books). It would make me very happy indeed if you were able to say something nice.

Thanks again,
Mark.

Printed in Great Britain
by Amazon